The Heart of Hyacinth

The Heart of Hyacinth

ONOTO WATANNA

Introduction by Samina Najmi

University of Washington Press

SEATTLE AND LONDON

Originally published by Harper & Brothers in 1903.
University of Washington Press paperback edition,
with a new introduction, published in 2000.
Introduction by Samina Najmi copyright © 2000
by the University of Washington Press.
All rights reserved.

Library of Congress Cataloging-in-Publication Data
Watanna, Onoto, 1879–1954.
The heart of Hyacinth / Onoto Watanna ;
introduction by Samina Najmi.
p. cm.
Includes bibliographic references (p.).
ISBN 0-295-97916-X
1. Japan—Race relations—Fiction.
2. Young women—Japan—Fiction.
3. Americans—Japan—Fiction.
4. Race relations—Fiction.
I. Najmi, Samina. II. Title.
PR9199.3.W3689 H42   2000
813í.52—DC21   99-059667

The paper used in this publication is acid-free and recycled
from 10 percent post-consumer and at least 50 percent
pre-consumer waste. It meets the minimum requirement
of American National Standard for Information Sciences
—Permanence of Paper for Printed Library Materials,
ANSI Z39.48–1984. ⊗ ♻

INTRODUCTION

WINNIFRED EATON, a woman of Anglo-Chinese ancestry who used the penname Onoto Watanna, wrote at the turn of the twentieth century, a time of intense sinophobia in the United States. Although most Chinese immigrants were seduced from China first by the Gold Rush and then by tales of fabulous employment opportunities on the American transcontinental railroad, once in the United States they found themselves not only doing backbreaking and dangerous work for little pay but discriminated against racially. Myths about the "heathen Chinee" abounded: on one hand, they were mysterious and unknowable; on the other, they were stereotyped as lagging far behind Caucasians on the evolutionary scale. They

Photo credit: Winnifred Eaton Reeve fonds, Special
Collections, 299/82.13, University of Calgary Library

were seen by whites as sneaky, dirty, smelly people who wore their hair in queues, ate disgusting things like rats, shrimp, and abalone, devoted themselves to gambling and prostitution, and spread diseases.

It has been suggested that between 1870 and 1905, the Chinese became San Francisco's "medical scapegoats": "Increasingly, the fear was expressed that the Chinese were carriers of alien disease that would ultimately cause the physiological decay of the American nation."[1] Such sentiments were so widespread that "the Chinese issue" had the power to influence votes for political office. In 1862, when Leland Stanford (who later founded Stanford University) became governor of California, he declared in his inaugural address: "To my mind it is clear, that the settlement among us of an inferior race is to be discouraged by every legitimate means. Asia, with her numberless millions, sends to our shores

1. Joan Trauner, "The Chinese as Medical Scapegoats in San Francisco 1870–1905," quoted in Rachel Lee (1997), p. 271.

the dregs of her population" (quoted in See 1995:8; M. Wong 1995:60). Although, as president of the Central Pacific Railroad, Stanford later realized how profitable it was to hire Chinese laborers, his words reflect the mood of the times.

In California, where the Chinese were a visible minority, a series of laws aimed at harassing them specifically forbade ironing after dark, levied taxes on laundrymen who carried clothes on poles, and limited the size of shrimp nets. But the discrimination against them was also codified by federal law. In 1870, the year in which the transcontinental railroad was completed, the Alien Land Act prohibited the ownership of land by the Chinese, among other Asians. Then, in 1882, came the Chinese Exclusion Act, the only immigration act ever to target a specific racial group (M. Wong 1995:62), which barred all Chinese laborers from entering the country. The policy of exclusion thrived until 1943, and during its fifty-year sway other legislative acts (in 1921 and 1924) insured that Chinese wives of American-born Chinese men were also denied entry to the United States. Anti-miscegenation laws existed in most states, making normal family life and population growth in the Chinese community virtually impossible.

Chinese exclusion was thus both economic and sexual, catering to labor fears that the Chinese were taking away jobs that rightfully belonged to white men and to white supremacist fears that Chinese men would marry white women. At California's constitutional convention in 1878, John F. Miller declared: "Were the Chinese to amalgamate at all with our people, it would be the lowest, most vile and degraded of our race, and the result of that amalgamation would be a hybrid of the most despicable, a mongrel of the most detestable that has ever afflicted the earth" (quoted in Takaki 1990:101). California's anti-miscegenation laws remained in effect until 1948. Although many discriminatory laws also affected groups other than the Chinese, nineteenth-century hysteria regarding the "yellow peril" centered mostly on them, as the most visible Asian group.[2]

Curiously, however, coexisting with this blatant racial discrimination was a certain fascination for Asia, which has come to be known as Orientalism, after Edward Said's famous book by that name. As Rachel Lee points out in her account of journalistic representations of Asian Americans at the turn of the century (1997), the media perpetuated negative stereotypes of Asians at the same time that they advertised "Oriental" products as exotic and desirable. Drawing on Said's idea of the "domestication of the exotic," Lee makes a provocative argument:

> While negative images of the Orient encouraged an American readership to be wary of Asian peoples, the commodification of

2. For detailed analyses of yellow perilism, past and present, see Thompson 1978, Wu 1982, and Okihiro 1994. Also, see Gina Marchetti, *Romance and the "Yellow Peril"* (1993), for an examination of Hollywood's depictions of miscegenation involving Asians and Caucasians.

the Orient into saleable product abated this sense of vulnerability. . . . Thus fear of Asians promoted by journalistic copy resulted not only in vociferous protest against social integration with Asians but also in readerly pleasure at seeing and consuming Asiatic commodities. (1997:254–56)

These twin reactions of hatred and exoticization were not targeted evenly at Asian groups. While the Chinese were vilified, in the first quarter of the twentieth century "positive" Orientalist sensibilities focused mostly on Japan, perhaps from awe of its military might, which had not yet become threatening to the United States. Moreover, the Japanese were not a visible minority in the late nineteenth century. Those who came to the United States quickly adopted Western manners of dress, unlike the Chinese (Kim 1982:125). Hence, according to S. E. Solberg,

The Chinese were commonly perceived as mysterious, evil, nearby, and threatening, while the Japanese were exotic, quaint, delicate (or manly, as the samurai), and distant. . . . The general fascination with the exotic (Japan) was able to transcend racist ideas so long as distance was a part of the formula." (1981:31–32)

Even as Chinese Americans and some Japanese Americans were ill treated on the home front, the "Orient"—specifically, Japan—figured in mainstream America's imaginings as a mysterious, exotic place: a land of temples and cherry blossoms, peopled by beautiful, glamorous but subservient geisha girls, and heroic samurais who preferred suicidal glory to defeat and dishonor.

Onoto Watanna responded to America's sinophobia by taking advantage of these Orientalist myths. Instead of either passing as white (as a person with her features could have done) or accepting the Chineseness imposed on someone of her heritage by the dominant culture, she chose not only to pass as a Eurasian of Japanese descent but, as Onoto Watanna,[3] actually to exploit the Orientalist fantasies of her readership to become a best-selling author.

Born Lillie Winnifred[4] Eaton in 1875 in Montreal, Canada, Onoto Watanna was the daughter of Grace Trefusis, a Chinese woman, and Edward Eaton, a part-Irish Englishman. In the early 1870s, the family had moved from England to Montreal, where Winnifred spent the first twenty years of her life. Edward Eaton (1839–1915), formerly a silk merchant, worked in Montreal as a clerk and bookkeeper until he decided to devote himself to his painting. With a new child born every year, the Eatons' fortunes declined rapidly, and the older children became part of a family work force. Grace Eaton (1846–1922), who was trained as a teacher, took it upon herself to

3. For an analysis of Eaton's chosen pseudonym, see Matsukawa 1994a).

4. Although, as Annette White-Parks points out, the name is spelled "Winifred" on the birth certificate, most scholars spell it "Winnifred," as did Watanna herself when she used her given name.

educate her children. As Annette White-Parks observes, "The closely monitored home education of all of the daughters is evident in their achievements, most impressively illustrated when Grace [Winnifred's older sister] becomes a lawyer" (1995:24). At least four of the Eaton children also inherited their father's artistic bent. Besides Winnifred, the novelist, there were two painters: Sara, the aspiring artist whose story forms the basis of Watanna's novel *Marion* (1916), and May, whose paintings on china still exist, along with a portrait of Winnifred.[5] Winnifred's eldest sister, Edith Maude Eaton, was destined for fame in ways similar to and yet very different from Winnifred.[6] Writing as

5. I am indebted to Diana Birchall for this information.

6. See White-Parks's book-length biography of Sui Sin Far (1995). Aside from the autobiographical writings of Watanna and Sui Sin Far, I draw heavily on White-Parks and Amy Ling (1990) for information regarding Watanna's family background. I am particularly grateful to Watanna's granddaughter, Diana Birchall, for helping me sift fact from fiction in varied accounts of Watanna's life and family.

INTRODUCTION

Sui Sin Far, Edith Eaton's autobiographical essay, "Leaves from the Mental Portfolio of a Eurasian" (1909), voices the pain and difficulty of growing up half Chinese in North America, even though, despite their keen awareness of their physical difference, the Eatons were not culturally Chinese. Their mother had been raised by English missionaries and the children grew up speaking English at home and were nurtured on Western classics. Most of the Eaton children eventually passed as white.

Artistically inclined, Winnifred felt acutely the privations of poverty in the cramped quarters of her home:

> I was the one who had to mind the children—the little ones; they were still coming—and I hated and abhorred the work. I remember once being punished in school because I wrote this in my school exercise: "This is my conception of hell: a place full of howling, roaring, fighting, shouting children and babies. It is supreme torture to a sensitive soul to live in such a Bedlam. Give

me the bellowings of a madhouse in preference. At least there I should not have to dress and soothe and whip and chide and wipe the noses of the crazy ones." (*Me*, 1997:113–14)

Watanna found her way out of the house when, at twenty, she left for Jamaica to work as a reporter for the *News Letter*. But she soon moved from there to Chicago, where she supported herself as a stenographer. It was here that she wrote *Miss Numè of Japan: A Japanese American Romance*, published in 1899 and to date the first known Asian American novel. Shortly thereafter, Watanna relocated to New York, where she would publish most of her novels.

In 1901, she married Bertrand Whitcomb Babcock, a news reporter, and had four children with him. Divorcing Babcock in 1916, she married Francis Reeve the following year. With Reeve she moved back to her native Canada, living on a cattle ranch in Calgary and producing three more novels. In 1924, she returned to the United States to try her hand as a scenarist in New York and Hollywood. The films she worked on include *Showboat, Phantom of the Opera, Shanghai Lady,* and *East Is West.* In 1931 she moved back to Calgary, where she lived until her death in April 1954.[7]

Miss Numè of Japan marked the beginning of an astounding career for Watanna. As *Harper's Weekly* noted in 1903, "Two years ago the name of Onoto Watanna was entirely unknown, except to a coterie in Chicago; today it is known everywhere" (Matsukawa 1994b). Between 1899 and 1925, Watanna wrote a memoir, a biography, and at least thirteen best-selling novels,[8] most of them romances set in Japan and all published by prestigious publish-

7. For detailed information on Watanna's career, I am indebted to Amy Ling (1990) and to Yuko Matsukawa's help and scholarship.

8. There is, apparently, a lack of critical consensus on the exact number of literary works by Watanna. While most scholars name thirteen to fifteen, Ling refers to Watanna's

ing houses. She was extremely successful in her lifetime. Many of her works were translated into a variety of languages, while her second novel, *A Japanese Nightingale* (1901), won praise from William Dean Howells[9] and, in 1903, ran briefly on Broadway.

In the 1940s, when it became preferable to be Chinese rather than Japanese, Watanna retracted her claim of Japanese ancestry. But to this day, she remains listed in *Who's Who*[10] as having been born in

---

"two dozen novels" (1992:309). Some of Watanna's novels brought her generous advances from the publishers (up to $15,000 in advance royalties), and her social circle included "such luminaries as Edith Wharton, Anita Loos, Jean Webster, David Belasco, Mark Twain and Lew Wallace" (Ling 1990:29).

9. In Howells's words, "There is a quite indescribable freshness like no other art except in the simplicity which is native to the best art everywhere," quoted in Ling 1990, p. 54. Ling also quotes a *New York Times* reviewer of *Tama* (1910), who describes the novel as "charmingly Japanese in form as well as in atmosphere . . . it holds the very spirit of Japan, a spirit fragrant, dainty, elusive."

10. *Who Was Who in America*, vol. 6; cited in Ling 1990, p. 36.

Nagasaki, Japan. To her credit, her novels have been praised in Japan for their astute portrayals of Japanese characters and for having the collective effect of a literary advertisement for Japan (Ling 1990:54; Doyle 1994:57). To her even greater credit, Otono Watanna was one of the few women writers in her time who was able to support herself and her family entirely with her pen.[11]

Watanna and American Literary Tradition

Watanna was a contemporary not only of William Dean Howells but also of Henry James and Edith Wharton, who, for most literary scholars and critics, represent the giants of American fiction at the turn of the twentieth century. Not surprisingly, James and Wharton emerge from a Eurocentric literary tradition, representing

11. See Elizabeth Ammons (1991) for an account of the link between gender and fiction writing at the turn of the twentieth century. Ammons's discussion includes Onoto Watanna specifically.

a specific, privileged race and class. Their art reflects an elite literary aesthetic, measured by which Watanna is found wanting: most of her novels are formulaic romances and, on the surface, simple in craftsmanship. However, as Nina Baym and others have shown, such criticism has been applied consistently to the works of many women writers and writers of color since the nineteenth century. Even highly influential authors such as Harriet Beecher Stowe have not always escaped charges of formulaic artlessness and sentimentality. Yet, as Jane Tompkins observes, one has only to glance at the history of anthologies to see how subjective such critical pronouncements are, being culturally and temporally specific. In *Sensational Designs*, Tompkins argues:

> The general agreement about which writers are great and which are minor that exists at any particular moment in the culture creates the impression that these judgments are obvious and self-evident. But their ob-

viousness is not a natural fact; it is constantly being produced and maintained by cultural activity: by literary anthologies, by course syllabi, book reviews, magazine articles, book club selections, radio and television programs, and even such apparently peripheral phenomena as the issuing of commemorative stamps in honor of Hawthorne and Dickinson, or literary bus tours of New England stopping at Salem and Amherst. (1985:193)

No one standard can be the sole yardstick for all art, especially when we consider that in the literary marketplace, as in academia, power relations—rather than "inherent" literary quality—frequently determine who gets published and who gets taught. Specifically, to be a woman writer of color at the turn of the twentieth century was to be doubly disadvantaged in the publishing arena. What Elizabeth Ammons says of Native American author Hum-ishu-ma (Mourning Dove) applies also to other women novelists of color during that time: "Edith Wharton's publication of seventeen novels and Hum-ishuma's publication of one . . . indicate how inextricable the issues of gender, race, class, ethnicity, and culture are in United States literary history" (Ammons 1991:282). That Onoto Watanna published almost as many novels as Wharton, then, represents a feat in itself.[12]

We can evaluate Watanna's contribution to American letters from a variety of perspectives. She racialized the popular romance, exploiting—in the age of American Realism—her audience's Orientalist fantasies, sexual and artistic. Ironically, she whose prolific writing fell out of favor for

12. Consider also Nina Baym's comment about women's best-selling romances, such as those Watanna wrote: "The idea of 'good' literature is not only a personal preference, it is also a cultural preference. . . . Until recently, only a tiny proportion of literary women aspired to artistry and literary excellence in the terms defined by their own culture. There tended to be a sort of immediacy in the ambitions of literary women leading them to professionalism rather than artistry, by choice as well as by social pressure and opportunity" (1992:5).

not being artful enough, constructed a highly marketable Japanese world without once having visited Japan. Both her personal life and her fiction challenge the concept of race as biological, positing instead the avant-garde notion that racial identities are socially constructed. In a career spanning the first quarter of this century, Watanna kept company not only with Henry James and Edith Wharton but also with such writers of color as Zitkala Sa, Charles Chesnutt, Pauline Hopkins, and James Weldon Johnson, the end of her writing career overlapping with the beginning of Nella Larsen's and Mourning Dove's. Strikingly, most of these authors were, like Watanna, of mixed racial heritage and in their writings explored the implications both of their biracial identities and of cross-racial encounters generally. Clearly, then, in the early twentieth century there was a burgeoning of coexistent and counter traditions to that represented by Wharton and James, which provide alternative contexts for Watanna's art. They demand our equal attention because, ultimately, at stake are not just questions of literary worth but questions of power. As Tompkins puts it: "The struggle now being waged in the professoriate over which writers deserve canonical status is not just a struggle over the relative merits of literary geniuses; it is a struggle among contending factions for the right to be represented in the picture America draws of itself" (1985:201). From this perspective, the context which most clearly illuminates Watanna's significance to American literary tradition is her contribution to Asian American literature.

Asian American Literary Pioneer

Until the publication of Watanna's *Miss Numè of Japan* in 1899, Asian American literature consisted mostly of short fiction, autobiography, and poetry.[13] Prior to 1899, much of this literature is specifically Chi-

13. For a detailed history of Asian American literature and its social contexts, see Kim 1982.

nese American, including that written in Chinese.[14] Among the published Asian American works written in English before 1925 (the year which marks the end of Watanna's active career) are personal accounts—written by "ambassadors of goodwill," as Elaine Kim calls them (1982:24)—such as Lee Yan Phou's *When I Was a Boy in China* (1887), Wu Tingfang's *America through the Spectacles of an Oriental Diplomat* (1914), and Japanese American Etsu Sugimoto's autobiographical novel, *A Daughter of the Samurai* (1925). In the area of Asian American—including Canadian—short fiction, Watanna's sister, Sui Sin Far, is generally held to be a pioneer, having published her first stories in 1888–89 (signed Edith Eaton) and her first "Chinese" stories in 1896, in the journal *Fly Leaf*

14. As Sauling C. Wong has shown, definitions of "Chinese American literature" are themselves problematic: if based on the author's residency in the United States, one would have to exclude works in English by Chinese writers who returned to China; for instance, Yung Wing's *My Life in China and America* (1909).

(White-Parks 1995:27, 30).[15] Unlike Watanna, Sui Sin Far chose to identify with Chinese Americans, exploding stereotypes about them in her writings and giving voice to their humanity and to the richness of their culture, as well as to the hardships and discrimination they faced in the United States. Her collection of short stories, *Mrs. Spring Fragrance* (1912), published two years before her death, has recently been reissued, and scholars such as Amy Ling (1992), Annette White-Parks (1995), and Elizabeth Ammons (1992) have de-

---

15. As Doyle points out, it is problematic to claim Sui Sin Far as Asian *American,* unless the term specifically includes Canadians. Although most of her works were published in the United States and this country forms the locale of most of her stories, Sui Sin Far spent only sixteen years of her life in the United States. For the theoretical implications of claiming Sui Sin Far as American, see David Shih, "The Seduction of Origins: Sui Sin Far and the Race for Tradition." Certainly, such considerations also apply to Watanna, mitigated in her case by the fact that her prolific career was a phenomenon of her almost thirty-year residence in the States. As Gail Jao observes in "Factual Fiction/Fictional Facts," Watanna herself emphasized her Americanness or her Canadianness as expediency dictated.

voted considerable critical attention to her stories. As far as the Asian American *novel* is concerned, however, to date we know of no publication prior to Watanna's *Miss Numè of Japan;* indeed, throughout the first quarter of the twentieth century, Watanna remains a rare Asian American writer to devote her energies to the genre of the novel.

Watanna's novels hit the U.S. literary marketplace with ornate covers and "Oriental" designs on every page. Most are romances with happy endings, although a few—*The Honorable Miss Moonlight* (1912) and, especially, *Cattle* (1923) and *His Royal Nibs* (1925)—reflect Watanna's talent as a literary realist. (The latter two, published under her given name, are set in Canada and make no attempt at an exotic effect in form or content.) *The Diary of Delia* (1907) forms another notable exception, being written in a surprisingly authentic Irish voice. In all cases, Watanna's heroines are feisty characters who, as Ling points out, begin at a social disadvantage but do more than survive through a combination of beauty and quick-witted resourcefulness. Frequently motherless and sisterless, they are free of immediate role models and, as such, their improvisations and breaches of convention appear justifiable or, at least, forgivable. Many enter into cross-racial relationships or are themselves biracial. In an era of anti-miscegenation laws, this thematic preponderance is radical, but Watanna makes the provocation palatable by staging her romances in a faraway land and casting the couple as white male–Asian female rather than the other way around (see also Ling 1990). In three novels she does engage the taboo subject of sexual relationships between white *women* and Japanese men. *Miss Numè of Japan* explores an abortive relationship between a Japanese Harvard graduate and a white American coquette. The young white widow in *A Japanese Blossom* (1906) marries a Japanese widower and together their families form an idyllic interracial Brady Bunch. But far more radical than either of these is *The*

Heart of Hyacinth (1903), as the reader will see.

Watanna also contributed to the form of memoir writing with *Me: A Book of Remembrance* (1915) and to biography with *Marion: The Story of an Artist's Model* (1916), co-authored with her sister Sara Bosse. To both these genres Watanna gives a trickster-like twist, creating highly selective, fictionalized accounts of her sister's life and her own and evading all discussion of the protagonists' Chinese ancestry. Unlike Sui Sin Far's autobiographical "Leaves," *Me* and *Marion* present the hardships of the protagonists' childhood and early youth as stemming entirely from poverty and having nothing to do with race. Indeed, in her memoir, despite occasional references to her dark hair and eyes, Watanna goes out of her way to identify with white womanhood, describing her experiences in Jamaica in blatantly racist terms.[16] Perhaps because

16. For more detailed discussions of *Me,* see Ling 1990, Matsukawa 1994a, Moser 1997, and Botshon (n.d.).

of this identification with white femininity, both *Me* and *Marion* were "successful in their day for their representations of the liberated 'new woman'—a character much closer in temperament to Winnifred herself" (Doyle 1994:55).

Given that Watanna was such a prolific, best-selling author in her own time, the question arises as to why her popularity among contemporary feminist literary critics has lagged so far behind her sister's. Certainly, her formulaic romances have not fared well in debates over aesthetic quality, which may account for the lack of interest in her works on the part of feminist scholars, professors, and publishers, in an era when numerous women writers were being rediscovered through their efforts. Along with scholars such as Baym and Tompkins, however, I would argue that it is shortsighted to dismiss the popular genre of the romance as unworthy of serious study, given that both its authors and its audience continue to be almost entirely women. Contrary to the popular belief that romances are solely an escape for house-wives, 40 to 60 percent of the 14 million women reading them work outside the home (Rabine 1985:165, 169). Moreover, as Leslie Rabine points out, "mass market romances are an international phenomenon . . . being translated into as many as fourteen languages" (1985:206).

Scholars have observed the contradiction that romances and romance-reading protest the established social order and, specifically, woman's marginalized place within it, but only just enough to appease women's genuine dissatisfactions, thereby preserving the status quo. Although I agree that romances ultimately tend to preserve rather than subvert patriarchal power structures, they do represent a limited rebellion—perhaps the only kind accessible to many women. As Janice Radway suggests, in their privileging of traditionally "female values of love and personal interaction," romances may be seen as a "collectively elaborated female ritual through which women explore the consequences of their common social condition" (Radway 1984:212). But even on the level of popular culture, romance reading is marginalized:

> While the masculine cultural pastime of equal popularity, the spectator sport of football, is shown on prime-time television, reading romances remains a quasi-secret activity for many readers. To read the cultural form which today shelters romantic ideals and desires is . . . generally regarded with scorn." (Rabine 1985:188)

Whatever their opinion of it as a literary form, the neglect of this genre by feminist critics, then, smacks of internalized misogyny—a charge against romance readers themselves, ironically. What Rabine says of romantic love also applies to the genre of the best-selling romance, in Watanna's time as in our own: "Instead of being scorned, it needs, like the heroines in the romances of old, to be liberated from captivity in the tower of patriarchal and corporate manipulation, but not by a Prince

Charming" (Rabine 1985:190).[17]

But there is another reason for Watanna's slow comeback in literary arenas today: in keeping with her trickster role, she slips through the cracks of contemporary multicultural agendas. Specifically, the brand of multiculturalism that flourishes in literary and academic circles today demands that ethnicity be the hallmark of "minority" writers—that these authors not only be catalogued according to their ethnic origin but that their own ethnicity be a conspicuous concern in their works.[18] Colluding in this expectation, feminist and Asian American literary critics often simply ignore Watanna, not knowing what else to do with her. Apart from the problems

17. Going further back, the influence of women's popular fiction on "high art," such as that of Henry James and William Dean Howells, is well-established. See, for instance, Ammons 1991.

18. Rajini Srikanth and Lavina Shankar take Asian American Studies to task for this (2000). See also Eve Oishi's "Introduction" to the reissue of *Miss Numè of Japan,* addressing similar reasons for Watanna's obscurity, and two

posed by her blithe fanning of Orientalist stereotypes, most Chinese Americans dismiss Watanna because she is not avowedly Chinese in her identification or her literary concerns. To most Japanese Americans, her biological heritage makes her a fake Japanese. As Matsukawa puts it, "In choosing to write as Onoto Watanna, Winnifred Eaton crosses the cultural lines to challenge what we perceive as the conventional boundaries of ethnicity and authenticity" (Matsukawa 1994a). It is a challenge we still seem unwilling to engage. Thus the astonishing fact that, despite a few pioneering efforts at recovery, most histories of Asian American literature do not so much as mention Watanna, preferring to leave un-

related essays: Christopher Douglas, "Reading Ethnography: Chinese American Fiction and the Legacy of Jade Snow Wong's *Fifth Chinese Daughter*," for an account of the origins and politics of ethnographic readings of Chinese American women's works, and Dominika Ferens, "Winnifred Eaton/Onoto Watanna: Establishing Ethnographic Authority," discussing Watanna's own intervention in the ethnographic writings of her time.

named and unclaimed its first and, until 1925, possibly only novelist.

Though Watanna has yet to make a complete comeback, the process of rediscovery has begun, as evidenced in literary circles such as the 1996 MLA Convention, the 1997 MELUS International Conference, and the 1999 and 2000 AAAS Conferences, which included entire panels on Watanna. Since the 1980s, there has been a steady rise in scholarship on her, leading to two recent republications of Watanna's works by academic presses: *Me* in 1997 and *Miss Numè of Japan* in 1999, as well as a forthcoming biography of Watanna's life by her granddaughter, Diana Birchall. Because of her historical importance as Asian America's first novelist, Watanna's resurgence is not surprising. Today's intellectual climate, moreover, permits us to acknowledge Watanna as a literary pioneer with a new measure of pride. At a time when the talk is of literary tricksters and subversive survivors, we can be not only more sympathetic but also more respectful toward

Watanna's strategic choice to pass as Japanese and her ability to market herself so profitably as a writer without ever visiting Japan.

The Heart of Hyacinth (1903)

The time is particularly ripe for interest in *The Heart of Hyacinth,* which is among the most "contemporary" of turn-of-the-twentieth-century novels and radical on many fronts. First, in an era when miscegenation was often illegal and always taboo, the novel not only racializes the popular romance (as do Watanna's other works), but it dares to represent a white woman's romantic/sexual relationships with Asian men. At the same time, in the character of the half-English Komazawa, Watanna probes the complexities and implications of biracial identity. And even more strikingly, the novel questions the very concept of biological race—a subject that has only recently received serious attention from social theorists.[19] Drawing on her own experience of race as malleable and socially constructed, Watanna creates in her protagonist a young white woman who, having grown up in Japan, not only claims a Japanese identity but shifts between her Japaneseness and her whiteness as expediency dictates, using her sense of racial plasticity to counter patriarchal claims, Caucasian and Japanese. In short, not only is *The Heart of Hyacinth* on the cutting edge of what we now call race theory, but that theory—of racial constructions and fluidity—is used in the service of an avant-garde feminism.[20]

Finally, with regard to audience, *The Heart of Hyacinth* on the one hand appeals as an easy-to-read romance and coming-of-age story; on the other, the issues it

19. See, for instance, Omi and Winant 1986, 1994, Gates 1986, Frankenberg 1993, and Lopez 1994.

20. For a fuller analysis of the novel, see my essay, "Racial Fluidity as Rebellion in Onoto Watanna's *The Heart of Hyacinth*," 2000.

engages make it an important teaching text not only in Asian American literature but in other academic arenas, such as Cultural Studies, Women's Studies, American Studies, and Ethnic Studies, to name a few. This reprint of Watanna's novel by the University of Washington Press—almost a century after its first publication—takes its place among other significant recovery projects in recent years. Reissues of writings by women and especially by women of color—Pauline Hopkins, Maria Ruiz de Burton, Zitkala Sa, and Sui Sin Far, for instance—illustrate that texts which for decades were not deemed important enough to remain in print can, in an intellectually receptive climate, be hailed as significant, pioneering works.

At the threshold of the twenty-first century, race reveals itself to be a social construct, as *The Heart of Hyacinth* so well demonstrates; but socially constructed, too, are judgments of literary worth, being contingent upon the vagaries of readers, critics, and publishers in a specific historical moment. In an ironic twist of literary fate, *The Heart of Hyacinth,* apparently over-simple in theme and plot, is rediscovered to have been theoretically far too sophisticated for its time.

Works Cited

Ammons, Elizabeth. "Gender and Fiction." In *The Columbia History of the American Novel,* ed. Emory Elliott, pp. 267–84. New York: Columbia University Press, 1991.

—. *Conflicting Stories: American Women Writers at the Turn into the Twentieth Century.* New York: Oxford University Press, 1992.

Baym, Nina. *Feminism and American Literary History.* New Brunswick, NJ: Rutgers University Press, 1992.

Birchall, Diana. *Her: The Story of Onoto Watanna.* Champaign: University of Illinois Press, 2000.

Botshon, Lisa. "Winifred Eaton: 'A Life of Not Unjoyous Deceit.'" In "Pretending to Be Me: Ethnic Transvestism and Cross-Writing," ed. Joseph Lockard and Melinda Micco. Manuscript.

INTRODUCTION

Douglas, Christopher. "Reading Ethnography: Chinese American Fiction and the Legacy of Jade Snow Wong's *Fifth Chinese Daughter*." In *Locating Asian American Literature in Intercultural Spaces*, ed. Samina Najmi and Zhou Xiaojing. Manuscript.

Doyle, James. "Sui Sin Far and Onoto Watanna: Two Early Chinese-Canadian Authors," *Canadian Literature* 140 (Spring 1994):50–58.

Ferens, Dominika. "Winnifred Eaton/Onoto Watanna: Establishing Ethnographic Authority." In *Locating Asian American Literature in Intercultural Spaces*, ed. Samina Najmi and Zhou Xiaojing. Manuscript.

Frankenberg, Ruth. *White Women, Race Matters: The Social Construction of Whiteness*. Minneapolis: University of Minnesota Press, 1993.

Gates, Henry Louis, Jr., ed. *"Race," Writing, and Difference*. Chicago: University of Chicago Press, 1986.

Jao, Gail. "Factual Fiction/Fictional Facts: The Life and Career of Onoto Watanna." Manuscript.

Kim, Elaine. *Asian American Literature*. Philadelphia: Temple University Press, 1982.

Lee, Rachel C. "Journalistic Representations of Asian Americans and Literary Responses, 1910–1920." In

INTRODUCTION

An Interethnic Companion to Asian American Literature, ed. King-Kok Cheung, pp. 249–73. New York: Cambridge University Press, 1997.

Lee Yan Phou. *When I Was a Boy in China.* Boston: D. Lothrop Company, 1887.

Ling, Amy. "Winnifred Eaton: Ethnic Chameleon and Popular Success," *MELUS* 11, 3(1984):5–15.

—. *Between Worlds: Women Writers of Chinese Ancestry.* New York: Pergamon Press, 1990.

—. "Creating One's Self: The Eaton Sisters." *Reading the Literatures of Asian America,* ed. Shirley Lim and Amy Ling, pp. 305–18. Philadelphia: Temple University Press, 1992.

Lopez, Ian Haney. "The Social Construction of Race: Some Observations on Illusion, Fabrication, and Choice," *Harvard Civil Rights-Civil Liberties Law Review* 29, 1(1994):1–62.

Marchetti, Gina. *Romance and the "Yellow Peril": Race, Sex, and Discursive Strategies in Hollywood Fiction.* Berkeley: University of California Press, 1993.

Matsukawa, Yuko. "Cross-Dressing and Cross-Naming: Decoding Onoto Watanna." In *Tricksterism in Turn-of-the-Century U.S. Literature,* ed. Elizabeth Ammons and Annette White-Parks, pp. 106–25. Hanover: University Press of New England, 1994a.

—. "Eaton, Winnifred." In *Reference Guide to American Literature,* ed. Jim Kamp, pp. 285–86. Detroit: St. James Press, 1994b.

Moser, Linda Trinh. Afterword to *Me: A Book of Remembrance,* by Winnifred Eaton/Onoto Watanna, pp. 357–72. Jackson: University Press of Mississippi, 1997.

Najmi, Samina. "White Woman in Asia: Racial Fluidity as Rebellion in Onoto Watanna's *The Heart of Hyacinth.*" In *Literary Studies East and West,* ed. Cynthia Franklin et al. Honolulu: University of Hawaii Press and East-West Center, 2000.

Oishi, Eve. Introduction to *Miss Numè of Japan,* by Onoto Watanna, pp. xii–xxxi. Baltimore: Johns Hopkins University Press, 1999.

Okihiro, Gary. *Margins and Mainstreams: Asians in American History and Culture.* Seattle and London: University of Washington Press, 1994.

Omi, Michael, and Howard Winant. *Racial Formation in the United States from the 1960s to the 1990s.* Originally published in 1986; reprint, New York: Routledge, 1994.

Rabine, Leslie. *Reading the Romantic Heroine: Text, History, Ideology.* Ann Arbor: University of Michigan Press, 1985.

INTRODUCTION

Radway, Janice. *Reading the Romance: Women, Patriarchy, and Popular Literature.* Chapel Hill: University of North Carolina Press, 1984.

Said, Edward. *Orientalism.* New York: Pantheon Books, 1978.

See, Lisa. On Gold Mountain: *The One-Hundred Year Odyssey of My Chinese-American Family.* New York: Vintage, 1995.

Shih, David. "The Seduction of Origins: Sui Sin Far and the Race for Tradition." In *Locating Asian American Literature in Intercultural Spaces,* ed. Samina Najmi and Zhou Xiaojing. Manuscript.

Solberg, S. E. "Sui Sin Far/Edith Eaton: First Chinese-American Fictionist," *MELUS* 8, 1(1981):27–39.

Srikanth, Rajini, and Lavina Shankar. "South Asian American Literature: 'Off the Turnpike' of Asian America." In *Postcolonial Theory and U.S. Ethnic Literature,* ed. Amritjit Singh and Peter Schmidt. Jackson: University Press of Mississippi, 2000.

Sugimoto, Etsu. *A Daughter of the Samurai.* Garden City, NY: Doubleday, 1925.

Sui Sin Far. "Leaves From the Mental Portfolio of a Eurasian," 1909. In *Mrs. Spring Fragrance and Other Writings,* ed. Amy Ling and Annette White-Parks, pp. 218–30. Urbana: University of Illinois Press, 1995.

Takaki, Ronald. *Strangers from a Different Shore: A History of Asian Americans.* Originally published in 1989; reprint, New York: Penguin, 1990.

Thompson, Richard. *The Yellow Peril, 1890–1924.* New York: Arno Press, 1978.

Tompkins, Jane. *Sensational Designs.* New York: Oxford University Press, 1985.

Watanna, Onoto. *Miss Numè of Japan: A Japanese-American Romance.* Originally published in 1899; reprint, Baltimore: Johns Hopkins University Press, 1999.

—. *A Japanese Nightingale.* New York: Harper & Bros., 1901.

—. *The Wooing of Wistaria.* New York: Harper & Bros., 1902.

—. *The Heart of Hyacinth.* Originally published in 1903; reprint, Seattle: University of Washington Press, 2000.

—. *Daughters of Nijo: A Romance of Japan.* 1904.

—. *The Love of Azalea.* New York: Dodd, Mead, & Co., 1904.

—. *A Japanese Blossom.* New York: Harper & Bros., 1906.

—. *The Diary of Delia.* New York: Doubleday, Page & Co., 1907.

—. *Tama.* New York: Harper & Bros., 1910.

—. *The Honorable Miss Moonlight.* New York: Harper & Bros., 1912.

—. *Me: A Book of Remembrance.* Originally published in 1915; reprint, Jackson: University Press of Mississippi, 1997.

—. *Marion: The Story of an Artist's Model.* 1916.

—. *Sunny-San.* New York: George H. Doran Co., 1922.

—. *Cattle* (as Winnifred Eaton). New York: A. L. Burt Co., 1923.

—. *His Royal Nibs* (as Winnifred Eaton Reeve). New York: W. J. Watt & Co., 1925.

White-Parks, Annette. *Sui Sin Far/Edith Maude Eaton: A Literary Biography.* Champaign: University of Illinois Press, 1995.

Wong, Morrison. "Chinese Americans." In *Asian Americans: Contemporary Trends and Issues,* ed. Pyong Gap Min, pp. 58–94. Thousand Oaks, CA: Sage Publications, 1995.

Wu Tingfang. *America Through the Spectacles of an Oriental Diplomat.* New York: Frederick S. Stokes, 1914.

INTRODUCTION

Wu, William. *The Yellow Peril: Chinese Americans in American Fiction, 1850–1940*. Hamden, CT: Archon Books, 1982.

Yung Wing. *My Life in China and America.* Originally published in 1909; reprint, New York: Arno, 1978.

The Heart of Hyacinth

THE HEART OF HYACINTH

I

THE City of Sendai, on the north-eastern coast of Japan, raises its head queenly-wise towards the sun, as though conscious of its own matchless beauty and that which envelops it on all sides. Here, where the waters flow into the Pacific, the surges are never heard. Neptune seems to have forgotten his anger in the presence of such peerless beauty.

Near to Sendai there is a bay called Matsushima. Here Nature has flung out her favors with more than lavish hand; for throughout the bay she has scattered jewel-like rocks, whose white sides rise above the waters, and whose surface gives nutrition to the graceful pine - trees which find their roots within the stone. Near to a thousand rocks they are said to number, and save for the one called Hadakajima, or Naked Island, all are crowned with pine-trees.

The historic temple Zuiganjii is situated at the base of a hill a few cho from the beach. About the temple are the tombs and sepulchres of the great Date family, once the feudal lords of Sendai. There is a huge image of Date Masamune, whose far-seeing mind sent an envoy to Rome early in the seventeenth century. The sepulchres are, for the most part, in the hollowed caves of the range of rocky hills behind the temples. Nameless flowers, large and brilliant in color, bloom about the tombs of these proud, slumbering lords. Mount Tomi bends its noble head in homage towards the glories of a past generation. The air is very still and cool. Silence enshrines and deifies all.

The inhabitants of Sendai and the

little fishing village on the northern shore of the bay were simple, gentle folk. As though affected by the slumbrous beauty of the hills and mountains hedging them in upon all sides, these let their life glide by with slow and sweetly sleepy tread. Not even the shock of the Restoration had brought this region's people into that prophetic regard for the future which pervaded all other parts of the empire. The change-compelling progress which pressed in upon all sides seemed not as yet to have laid its withering finger upon fair Matsushima. Like their home, the inhabitants clung to their hermit existence.

When an English ship, having ploughed its way through the waters of the Pacific, sent out its men in boats to take the bay's soundings, the people were not alarmed, but greatly mystified. The strange white men made their way in their smaller boats to the shore. A missionary and his wife were landed.

A little home, on a small hill situated

3

only a short distance from the Temple Zuiganjii, they built for themselves. Afterwards, native artisans raised for them a larger structure, where for many years they patiently taught the gospel of Jesus Christ. The people gradually learned to love and reverence their pale teachers. There came a time when the little band, which had at first gone desultorily and curiously to the mission-house, began to see what the strangers termed "the light." Then the Christian Church in far-away England enrolled a little list of converts to their religion.

The missionary grew old and white and bent. His gentle wife passed away. He lingered wistfully, a strangely isolated, though beloved, figure in the little community.

Then came a second visitation from an English vessel. Sailors and officers lolled about the town by day and rioted by night. Some of them wooed the dark-eyed daughters of the town but to leave them. One there was, however, who brought a girl, a shrinking, yet trustful girl, to the old missionary on the hill, and there, in the shabby old mission-house, the solemn and beautiful ceremony of the Christian marriage service was performed over their heads.

That was ten years before. At first the Englishman had seemingly settled in his adopted land, as he loved to call it. The place appealed to his artistic perceptions. The Mecca of all his hopes, he called it. Why should he return to the world of cold and strife? Here were peace, rest, and love unbounded. But before the close of the second year of their union an event occurred which shook the stranger suddenly into life's vivid reality. A great duty thrust itself in his track. Not for himself, but for another, must he turn his back upon the land of love. A son had been born to him in the season of Little Heat.

So the Englishman crushed to his breast his foreign wife and child, and with reiterated promises of a speedy return he left them.

Letters in those days travelled slowly from England to Japan. Sometimes those addressed to the little town of Sendai remained for weeks in the offices at the open ports. Sometimes they travelled hither and thither from one port to another, the stupid indifference of officials scarcely troubling itself to send them to their proper destination. But finally, after many months, the little wife and mother in Sendai held between her trembling hands an English letter. It had come in a very large envelope, and there were several bulky inclosures — neatly folded documents they were—tied with red tape. There was also another letter, shorter than the one she held in her hand, and written in a different form. She could not even read her letter, though she did not doubt from whom it had come. Happy, she pressed her precious package to her lips and breast. She believed that the

6

strangely printed papers within the envelopes, similar in her eyes to the many English papers he had always about him, were merely other forms of his epistle of love.

The woman waited with a divine patience for the return of the old missionary from a little journey inland. She watched for him, watched ceaselessly, constantly. And when he had returned she dressed the little Komazawa in fresh, sweet-smelling garments, and carried him with her papers to the mission-house.

Why detail the pain of that interview? The papers and one of the letters, it is true, were, indeed, from her lord, but they were sent by another, a stranger. The Englishman had died— died in what he termed a foreign country, since his home was by her side. In his last hours he had striven to write to her and instruct her in the course she must take in the years to come when he could not be by her as her loving guide.

7

Madame Aoi meekly followed the counsel of the aged missionary. Under his guidance, childlike and with unquestioning faith, she studied unceasingly the English language and the Christian faith.

If the old missionary had at first marvelled at the calm which settled upon her after that one wild outcry when first she had heard the dread tidings of her husband, he was not long in discovering that her passiveness was but an outer mask to veil the anguish of a broken heart, and to give her that strength which must overcome the weakness which would be the doom of her hopes. For Aoi was not left without some hope in life. Her lord, in departing, had set upon her an injunction, a duty. This it was her task to perform. Once that was accomplished, perhaps the strain might lessen. Meanwhile tirelessly, ceaselessly, she studied.

She had the natural gift of intelligence, and the advantage of having

8

spent two full years with her husband. Hence it was not long before she mastered the language, and, if she spoke it brokenly and even haltingly, she wrote and read accurately.

To the little Komazawa she spoke only in English. She kept him jealously apart from the villagers, and taught his little tongue to shape and form the words of his father's language.

"Some day, liddle one," she would say, "you will become great big man. Then you will cross those seas. You will become great lord also at that England. So! It is the will of thy august father."

II

It was the season of Seed Rain. The country was green and fragrant and the crops thirstily absorbed the rain. The villagers sat at their thresholds, some of them even indolently lounging in the open, unmindful or perhaps enjoying the seething rain, an antidote for the heat, which was somewhat sweltering for the season.

Children were playing in the street, nimbly jumping over the puddle ponds, or climbing, with the agility of monkeys, the trees that lined the streets, and about whose boughs they hung in various attitudes of daring delight.

One small boy had climbed to the very tip of a bamboo, and there he clung by his feet, swaying with the shakings of the slender tree, and the motion of those below him—far below him.

It was not often that the son of
Madame Aoi was permitted such ab-
solute freedom. Indeed, it was only
upon those occasions when Komazawa,
momentarily blind to the reproach of
his mother's sad eyes, literally thrust
away the bonds which seemed to hold
and chain him to their quiet household
and burst out and beyond their reach.
Surely, at the tip of this long, perilous
bamboo he was quite beyond the reach
of little Madame Aoi and her old servant, Mumè. But even in his present
lofty position Komazawa had kept his
eyes from the possible glimpse of his
mother. His feet clung to the tree only
because his hands were engaged in covering his ears.

Yet, even in the open, Komazawa was
alone. The neighbors' children played
in little bodies and groups together, and
Komazawa from his perch watched them
with the same ardent wistfulness with
which he was wont to regard them from
the door of his little isolated home.

Old Mumè was angry. Her voice had become hoarse, and she was tired of her position in the rain, for the bamboo gave but scant shelter. She shook the tree angrily.

"Do not so," entreated the gentle Aoi. "See how the tree bends. Take care lest it become angry with us and vent its vengeance upon my son. But, pray you, good Mumè, return to the home and give food and succor to our honorable guest."

As Mumè shuffled off, her heavy clogs clicking against the pavement, Aoi called up, entreatingly, to the truant:

"Ah, Koma, Koma, son, do pray come down."

But Komazawa, with head thrown backward, was whistling to the clouds. He was very well content, and it pleased him much to be wet through. How long he sat there, whistling softly strange airs and imagining wild and fanciful things, he could not have told, since the passage of time in these days of freedom was a thing which he noted little.

Gradually he became aware that the rain was becoming colder and the sky had darkened. Komazawa looked downward. There was nothing but darkness beneath him. He shivered and shook his little body and head, the hair of which was weighted with rain. Komazawa began to slide downward, feeling the way with his feet and hands. It was quite a journey down. In the darkness he had knocked his little shins against out-jutting broken boughs. He landed with both feet upon something palpitating and soft—something that caught its breath in a sigh, then inclosed him in its arms.

Komazawa guilty, but not altogether tamed, spoke no words to his mother. He stood stiffly and quietly still while she felt his wetness with her hands. But he threw off the cape in which she endeavored to wrap him. He was obliged to stand on tiptoe to put it back around his mother, and as this was an undignified position, his bravado broke down.

13

Gradually he nestled up against her, and
—strange marvel in Japan!—these two
embraced and kissed each other.

After a while, as they trudged silently
down the street homeward, Komazawa
inquired, in a sharp little voice, as he
looked up apprehensively at his mother:

"And the honorable stranger, mother?"

Aoi hesitated. The hand about her
son trembled somewhat. His thin little
fingers clutched it almost viciously. He
flushed angrily.

"Why do you not answer me?" he
asked, with peevishness.

"I have not seen the honorable one,"
said Aoi, gently.

"Pah!" snapped the boy. "No, certainly, and we do not wish to see her.
We do not like such bold intrusion."

"Nay, son," she reproved, "we must
not so regard it. Let us remember the
words of the good master, the august
missionary."

"What words?" inquired Koma, tart-

14

ly. "Why, his excellency does not even know of the coming of the woman, since he is gone three days from Sendai now."

"Ah, but my son, do you not remember that he taught us to treat with kindness the stranger within our gates?"

Koma made a sound of disapproval, his little, ill-tempered face puckered in a frown. After a moment he inquired again:

"But where is the woman, mother?"

Aoi regarded her small son almost apologetically.

"She is within our humble house," she replied.

Koma pulled his hand from hers with a jerk. For a time he walked beside her in silence. He was strangely old for his years, and already he showed the inheritance of his father's pride.

"Mother," he said, "we do not wish the stranger to disturb our home. My father would not have permitted it. We are happy alone together. What do we want with this woman stranger?"

"But, my son, she is very ill."

"She should have stayed at the honorable tavern. We do not keep a hostelry."

Aoi sighed.

"Well," she said, hopefully, "let us bear with her for a little while and afterwards—"

"We will turn her out," quickly finished the boy.

"We will entreat her to remain," said Aoi. "It would be proper for us to do so. But the stranger will not be lacking in all courtesy. She will not remain."

They had reached their home. Now they paused on the threshold, the mother regarding the son somewhat appealingly, and he with his sulky head turned from her. Aoi pushed the sliding-doors apart. A gust of wind blew inward, flaring up the light of the dim andon and then extinguishing it. The house was in darkness.

Suddenly a voice, a piercing, shrill voice, rang out through the silent house.

16

"The light, the light!" it cried; "oh, it is gone, gone!"

Koma clutched his mother's hand with a sudden, tense fear.

"The light!" he repeated. "Quickly, mother; the honorable one fears the darkness. Quickly, the light!"

III

OLD Mumè was busily engaged in the kitchen. The milk over the fire had begun to bubble. With a large wooden stick she stirred it. Then she returned to her rice. As she pounded it into flat cakes, her old face, with its hundred wrinkles, was contorted, and she muttered and talked to herself as she worked. She was like some old witch, breathing incantations.

At the threshold of the room stood Koma. His eyes were very wide open and his cheeks were flushed. At his side his little hands were sharply clinched. His whole attitude betokened excitement and impatience. Suddenly he clapped his hands so loudly and sharply that the old woman started in fright; then catching sight of the little intruder,

she hobbled towards him on her heels,
her tongue in angry operation.

"Now, who but an evil one would
frighten an old woman? Shame upon
you, naughty one!"

"Oh, Mumè, you are so slow the evil
one will catch you. Just see, the milk
boils over. Still you do not hasten.
Yet the illustrious ones are ill, very
ill."

"Tsh!" scolded the old woman, as she
poured the steaming milk into a shallow
bowl, and broke pieces of the rice-bread
into it. "What, would you advise old
Mumè about such matters? Would you
have me burn the honorable babe?"

She cooled the preparation with her
hand, fanning it back and forth across
the bowl.

Koma watched her a moment with
smouldering eyes. Suddenly he started,
his little ears alert and attentive.

A cry, thin and piping at first, grew
in volume. Was it possible that so small
a thing could fill the house with its

19

noise? Koma strode to the fire, seized the bowl with both hands, and, before the grumbling old servant could interfere, he was gone with it from the room, and speeding along the hall.

With his finger-tips on the closed shoji of the guest-chamber he tapped gently. It was softly pushed aside, and Aoi appeared in the opening. Stepping into the hall, she closed the sliding screens behind her.

The boy spoke in an eager whisper.

"Here is the milk the honorable one desired."

"Where did you obtain it, son?"

"In the village. And see, we have warmed it, for it was quite cold. It is good goat's milk."

"Such a good son!" whispered Aoi, and stooped to kiss the upraised face ere she returned to the sick-chamber.

Koma crouched down on the floor by the door. He could hear within the soft glide of his mother's feet across the floor. There was a murmuring of indistin-

guishable words. Then that voice, with
its strange accent, which seemed to
pierce and reach something in the boy.

The voice was weak now, but its exquisite clearness was not dulled. Then
Koma heard the movement of the lifting
of the babe; a little cry or two, then little
gurgling, satisfied gasps. The babe was
being fed with the milk he had procured.
It gave Koma a strange satisfaction—
a warm delight. He stretched out his
little limbs across the floor. He, too,
was satisfied. All was now well. Gradually his head drooped backward and
Komazawa fell into a slumber.

Within, the stranger was imparting
bits of her history to the sympathetic
Aoi. She was hardly conscious of her
words, which were spoken through her
semi-delirium. Her feverish eyes, wide
open, shone up into the bending face of
Aoi, and held the Japanese woman with
their piteous appeal. She seemed sooth-
ed under the gentle touch of Aoi's hand
on her brow.

"Pray thee to sleep," gently the Japanese woman persuaded her.

She was quiet a moment, only to start up the next.

"Nay," entreated Aoi, "sleep first—to-morrow speak. Rest, I pray you."

"It was so long, so long!" cried the woman on the bed, clasping her thin hands across those on her head. "And, oh, the pain, the agony of it all! I was so tired—so—"

Her body palpitated and quivered with the sighing sobs that shook her. She sprang up suddenly, pushing away from her the hands of Aoi, which gently attempted to restrain her.

"It was all wrong—quite wrong from the first. But what did they care? They had their wedding. Ah, I tell you, they are bad, all bad! Ah, it was cruel, cruel!"

"Ah," thought Aoi, sadly; "she, too, has been pierced with anguish. Truly, my heart breaks in sympathy with her."

She bent above the quivering woman, her pitying face close to hers.

"Pray thee, dear one, take rest and comfort," she said, smoothing softly her brow.

"Ah, you are so good, so good," said the sick woman. "You are not like those others—those fearful people." She covered her eyes with her thin hands as if to shut out a vision of some horror. "God will bless you, bless you for your goodness to me," she said.

Exhausted, she lay back among the pillows, her eyes closed. How grateful to her must have felt that great English bed, with its soft coverlets! For how many days had she wandered, without sight or word of her own people! Her thin, fine lips quivered unceasingly, while her blue eyes held a constant mist, seemingly haunted by some troubled spectre that pursued her ceaselessly.

Once she raised her hands feebly, then plucked at the coverlet with long, white fingers.

23

"What a death! oh, what a death!" she whispered, faintly.

After a long silence her voice raised itself to the pitch of one delirious.

"If I could see—" Her words came slowly and with difficulty, and she repeated them ramblingly. "If I could only see—a white face—a white—one of my own people. Oh, so long, and, oh me!—mamma, mamma!"

"Ah, dear lady," said Aoi, "if you will but deign to rest I will go forth and endeavor to find some of your people. There are white people in the next town. It is not far—not very far, and perhaps, ah, surely, they will come to you."

"My people," the woman repeated. "No, no." Her voice became hoarse. She started up in her bed. "You do not understand. I must never, never see them again. I could not bear it. They are cruel, wicked. No! Ah, you shall promise me—promise me."

She fell back, exhausted from her transport of passion. Aoi knelt beside

24

her and took her hands within her own.

"I will promise you whatever you wish, dear lady. Only speak your desires to me. I will humbly try to carry them out."

The sick woman's voice was so weak that she scarce could raise it above a whisper, but her words were plain.

"Promise me that you will not give them my little one when I am gone. You are good, and will be kind to her. Oh, will you not? I would not be happy, I could not rest in peace if she were sent to — to him." Her words rambled off again. "I left him," she said, "ran away—far away, far away, and the country was all strange to me, and I could not find my way. Every one stared at me; it must have been because I had gone mad, you know, quite mad. All women do. I wanted to put a great distance between us, to get beyond his sight—beyond the sound of his voice, beyond—"

25

"Ah, do not speak more," entreated Aoi, now in tears.

"Why, you are crying!" said the sick woman, looking wistfully into Aoi's face. She began to weep, weakly, impotently, herself.

After a time she became quieter. She started once again, when Aoi had snuffed a few of the lights, seeming to dread the darkness, but when the Japanese woman's hands reassured her, she was again silent. And as she slept she still clung spasmodically to the hands of Aoi.

IV

MORNING dawned with a haggard light. Ceaselessly the rain drizzled down. The torpid heat of the previous day had given place to a clammy chilliness. The weather oppressed the sick one. Her restlessness was gone, but passive quiet was more ominous. Her white face seemed to have shrunken through the night — so white and still it was that she seemed scarcely to breathe.

Too weak to bear the burden of her child against her, the mother permitted the little one to be cared for in an interior room lest its cries might disturb her. All through the day she spoke no word. Wearily, the heavy lids of her eyes were closed.

As the day began to wane, Aoi, thoroughly alarmed, summoned the vil-

lage doctor; a very old and learned man
he was considered. He felt the woman's hands, listened to her breathing with
his ear against her lips. Very cold her
hands were, but her breathing was reg-
ular, though faint.

The doctor looked grave, solemn, and
wise. He shook his bald head ominously.

"How long has the honorable one
been thus?"

"Since early morn, sir doctor. She
awoke from her night sleep only to fall
into this condition."

"The woman has but a short space of
life left to her," said the doctor, solemnly.

Aoi trembled.

"Her people—" she began, falteringly. "Oh, good sir doctor, it is very,
very sad. So young! Ah, so beautiful!"

Seeming not to share or understand
Aoi's sympathy, the doctor gathered
up his instruments and simples slowly,
meanwhile glancing uneasily towards

the face of the sick woman. He turned suddenly to Aoi.

"Madame," he said, "the village sympathizes with you at the infliction placed upon you by this enforced guest, but—"

"You do not finish, sir doctor?"

"The woman became a nuisance at the tavern. The people there were not Kirishitans (Christians), and were moreover in ignorance of the woman's speech. They could only comprehend that she wished to be taken to some one of her own people—so, madame, you—"

"I, being of her people," said Aoi, with simple dignity, "she was brought to me. That was right. I thank my neighbors for their kindness. I am honored, indeed, with such a guest. She is welcome."

The doctor moved towards the door.

"And the child? It is well, and will not accompany the mother on her last journey. What will become of it?"

Aoi did not reply.

29

"If it is desired by you, Madame Aoi," said the doctor, endeavoring to be kind, "I will immediately despatch word to the city to send notification to the nearest open port. There, surely, must be some consul, or representative of the woman's country. To them the child should go."

Aoi spoke swiftly.

"The poor one's people were unkind to her and cruel. How can we tell but that they might also abuse the child?"

"That is the affair of the child, Madame Aoi. Pray accept my counsel. Send the child—"

Interrupted by the sudden entrance of little Komazawa, he did not finish. The boy had evidently heard all, through the thin partition doors, against which he had leaned, listening intently. He thrust himself now before the doctor, with eyes purpled by excitement. His tense little body quivered.

"Sir doctor," he said, in a voice new even to his mother, it was so strong

and haughty, "you make mistake. The
child is already among its own people.
Here, in my father's house, all people are
Engleesh. So! The child belongs to us,
since the mother did present it to us.
It is a gift of the good God!"

Smiling and frowning together the little doctor bowed ironically to the little
fellow facing him.

"And will the august one enlighten
me as to whether he will make an effort
to find the child's legal guardians?"

"That is our affair, sir doctor, but I
will answer. We will ask advice of the
good excellency when he returns. He
is in Sendai even now. He will be in our
village to-night."

The doctor bowed himself out, and
Koma turned to his mother, a question
in his eyes. Aoi nodded sadly. The
poor white woman would die, had said
the sir doctor.

Komazawa approached the bed softly,
until he stood by the woman's side,
looking down fixedly upon her. How

31

white was the still face, how beautiful
the long lashes that swept the cheeks,
how wonderful and sunlike the silken
hair enveloping her head like a halo.
Could she be real, this beautiful, still
creature? Never had Komazawa seen
anything like her. She seemed a spirit
of the lingering twilight.

Suddenly he bent over her and softly
touched the small hand that lay outside
the coverlet. But soft as was his touch
it acted like an electric shock upon the
woman. She started and quivered, as
her heavy lids lifted. At the little face
bending above her she stared. A strange
expression came into her face. Her
voice was like that of one murmuring
in a dream.

"A little white boy," she said. "A
little white—"

Her lips were stilled, but a breath, a
sigh passed from her as Koma, with a
sudden instinctive motion, put his face
down to hers. When Aoi gently drew
the boy up she found the still, white

face softly smiling in the twilight, as though ere she slept she had seen a vision.

But Komazawa knelt by the bedside, weeping passionately.

V

NEAR the Temple Zuiganjii there is one huge rock, where the Date lords in the feudal days were wont to gather yearly, attended by musicians, and seeking recreation in gay amusements. It is of enormous size, and when the sun's rays beat upon its white surface it shines like white, polished glass. Flat, embedded in the soil, there is, however, a part of the rock which rises many feet above the level, its out-jutting point resembling the head of some giant sea-monster. Under this jutting head a natural cave has been formed.

Here, on a summer day, two children were playing together. Far below them the Bay of Matsushima spread out its insistent beauty. Moored to the beach, a few cho below them, was their miniature raft-sampan, an old weather-beaten boat, in which they had made their pilgrimage from the village. Behind them were the tombs and the eastern hills. The sunlight slanting upon them was no less golden than these summer foot-hills of the mountains beyond.

Bareheaded and barelegged the children were, the sandals upon their feet wet, showing how they had paddled in the bay. The boy, a lad of possibly fifteen years, was stretched full length under the shadow of the rock, only his sandalled feet projecting into the sunlight, which he hoped would dry them. His elbows were in the sand, his chin resting upon one arm. He was reading from a very much worn and ragged book, the leaves of which he turned with the utmost care and tenderness.

The little girl had gradually come from the rock's shadow, and now squatted at his feet. The sun fell upon her. She was a diminutive, odd little mite. Her hair, a dark shining brown, had been

carefully knotted up into a little chignon
at the top of her head, but, being way-
ward by nature, it had escaped the most
persistent brushing and the severe pins
which held it. It clung around her ears
and little neck in soft, damp curls. Her
face and hands were russet, sunburned
and freckled. Her eyes were large and
gray, shading towards blue. She wore
but one garment, a little red, ragged
kimono, very much frayed at the ends
and soaked from her late paddling. Unlike the average Japanese child, the little girl was restless and lacked all sense
of repose, an inherent instinct with Japanese children.

Though the boy had constituted her
his audience and was reading aloud to
her, she apparently had heard no word
of what he had been reading. Having
wriggled her way beyond the reach of his
hand, she now looked about her for new
means of engaging her active little mind.
This she discovered in some stalks of
grass. Having selected the stiffest blade

she could find, she stealthily crept back
to the feet of the boy, and first tickled,
then pricked his feet with the grass. The
natural result followed. The boy's dron-
ing, monotonous voice in reading changed to a sudden, sharp grunt, and he threw
up his heels, whereat the little girl burst
into a wild, elfish peal of laughter. At
the same time she renewed her jabs at
the boy's protesting feet.

Komazawa, still agitating his heels,
closed the book with care, placed it in
safety in the sleeve of his hakama, and
swung upward, drawing his heels under
him beyond the reach of his naughty
tormentor.

With assumed gravity he regarded the
small rogue before him.

"Something bitten you, yes?" she inquired, keeping her distance from him
and hugging her knees up to her chin.

Koma nodded, silently.

"What?" she inquired. "What was
that bitten you, Koma?"

"Gnat!" said the boy, briefly.

37

"Gnat?" She crept a few paces nearer to him, and peered up into his face.

"Yes—gnat," he repeated, "bad devil gnat."

The expression on the little girl's face was involved. How was it possible for any one ever to know just what Komazawa meant when his face was so grave and smileless. She had an odd little trick of glancing up at one sideways under her eyelashes. She peeped up at Koma now for some time in this manner. Her mirth had changed to a matter of speculation. Did or did not Koma know *what* had bitten him? He had said it was a gnat. Her intelligence was not sufficiently developed to include the possibility that he might have meant her for the gnat. She ventured:

"Did you see that gnat bite you?"

"Yes, twice."

Her eyes became wide.

"Where is it gone?" she inquired, breathlessly.

"Still there," was his reply.

38

" Where ?" She started, actually frightened. Koma's voice and air of mystery began to work upon her active imagination. What was a gnat, anyway? And if one had actually bitten Komazawa, might it not also bite her? By this time she had entirely forgotten her own attacks with the grass blade. She was close to Koma now, her hands upon his arm, her upraised eyes searching his face.

"What is a gnat, Komazawa?"

"Bad little insect."

"Oh! Does it bite?"

"Yes."

"Did it also bite you?"

"Three times."

"Oh!" A palpitating pause. Then:

"Will it bite me, too?"

"Maybe."

She crept completely into his arms, shielding herself with his sleeves.

"Where is it—that bad gnat?"

"Here." He pointed at her with an index-finger.

"Here!" She gave a little scream. "On my face!"

She was a small bundle of pricked nerves, frightened at a shadow of her own making. Komazawa relented, and pressed her little, fluttering face against his own.

"There — foolish one! No; there is nothing on your face. You are the gnat I meant."

"Me!" She drew back a pace. "But I am not an insect!"

"Little bit like one," said Koma, a smile of sunshine replacing his affected gravity a moment since.

His small companion sat up stiffly, half indignant, half curious.

"How'm I like unto an insect gnat?"

"Gnat jumps—this way, that, every way. So you do so. Can't sit still, listen to beautiful stories."

"I don't like those kind stories. Like better stories about ghosts and—"

"Oh, you always get afraid of such stories, screaming like sea-gull."

"Yes, but all same, I like to do that
—like to hear such stories—like also get
frightened and scream."

"Gnat also bites—bites foot, same as
you do."

"That don't hurt," she said, her eyes
askance. Then, repeating her words,
questioningly, "That don't hurt?"

"Oh yes, it does, certainly. What do
you suppose I got to keep my feet under
me now for?"

Her little bosom heaved.

"Let me see those foots, Komazawa."

"Too sore."

"Oh, Komazawa!"

Her eyes were beginning to fill. He
thrust his two feet out quickly.

"No, no; they are all right."

Her face was aglow again in an instant.

"Oh, I love you, my Koma," she said.
"I only pretend hurt your honorable
foots."

"That's right. Now, you fix your
hands so." He illustrated, doubling his

41

own hands into fists, then doubling hers also.

"That's right. Make hand good and hard. So! Now you hit hard against those feet. So!"

He brought her little, closed fist down hard with his own hand on his offending foot. The little girl became pale. Her lips quivered. She began to sob.

Koma lifted her in his arms, jumped her on his shoulder, and carried her down to the beach, soothing her as he walked.

"That's just little punishment for me; punishment for teasing little sister," said Koma, laughing quietly. "That don't hurt. You going to laugh soon? You just little gnat! That's so? You bite just little bit. I am big dog. I bite big."

He set her in the boat.

"Such a foolish little gnat," he said, "always cry—always laugh. Like these waters—sometimes jump—sometimes lie still."

42

Standing in the boat he pushed it out into the bay with the large pole which served as a sort of paddling oar.

He smiled back over his shoulder at her. "Ah, the wind go blowing us home so quick. Now you smile once more. Good! Sun come up again!"

He had been speaking to her in English, idiomatic, but clear. Now he broke into Japanese song. His voice was round and large, full and sweet for one so young. It seemed to ring out across the bay, and float back to them from the echoing hills.

VI

"Alas!" said Madame Aoi, as she brushed, with long hopeless strokes, the rippling hair of little Hyacinth. "Alas! no use try to keep you nice. Look at those hands—so brown like little boy's —and that neck and face!"

Hyacinth sat upon the weekly chair of torture. Her little russet face had been scrubbed till it shone. Her hair was being brushed uncomfortably smooth with water, to prepare it for being twisted up in a pyramid on her head. Had she been a properly regulated Japanese child, one such hair-dressing a month would have sufficed. But, as a rule, she had scarcely escaped from under the painstaking hands of Aoi before she managed to shake down, or at least

44

loosen, the beautiful glossy coiffure upon her head.

Cleaning - day, Hyacinth dreaded. Though Koma had taught her to swim in the bay like a veritable little duck, it is sad to relate that the little girl despised water which was thrown upon her for the purpose of removing that dirt, the inevitable portion of a child who plays continually in the open and burrows in beach sand.

So now, restless, rebellious, and miserable, anything but the usual passive little Japanese girl, she squirmed under the hands of Aoi.

The day was Sunday, a red-letter day for Aoi. The mission-house on the hill opened its doors to its tiny congregation upon this day. Hence Aoi prepared her little family against this weekly event, and poor Hyacinth was the chief subject of torture. Koma's hair grew in a short, smooth mass, which required no brushing or twisting. Also, he had reached an age when he had wholly graduated

45

from his mother's hands and was competent to effect his own toilet. But he was forced to sit in the chamber of horrors during the time that his sister was undergoing the weekly operation, since, were his presence removed, it would have been impossible to manage or control the restless child.

"There!" exclaimed Aoi, as she placed the last pin in the child's head. "Now, that is fine. Been good child to-day."

Hyacinth slid down from the small stool, lingered in discontent on the floor a moment, then, with an expression of childish resignation, rose to her feet and stood silently awaiting further operations upon her.

Aoi lightly wafted a little powder towards her face and neck; then removed it with a soft cloth. The tanned skin appeared whitened and softened. Then she dressed her little charge in a fresh crêpe kimono—a red-flowered kimono it was—tied a purple obi about it with a huge bow behind, placed a flower orna-

46

ment in the side of her hair, and Hyacinth's toilet was completed.

Her appearance did credit to the labor of Aoi. She seemed such a bewitching, quaint little figure—her face, piquantly pretty, her hair shining, the red flower ornament matching her little red cheeks and lips. A moment later, too, the discontent and restlessness had quite fled from her face, for Koma had seized her the instant of her release and given her an enormous hug, to the palpitating anxiety of Aoi, who besought him to be careful not to disturb the elegance of her hair and gown.

"Now," she told them, "go sit at the door like good children. Keep very still. Soon your mother will also be ready."

Aoi expended less pains upon her own person. Her hair erection needed no re-dressing. She changed her cotton kimono for a very elegant silken one, powdered her face lightly in a trice, and a moment later was at the door, anxiously looking about for the children.

47

She was still a young woman, so pretty that it was hard to believe her the mother of a boy of sixteen. Her figure was slight and girlish, her face unmarked by any trace of age, save that the eyes were sad and anxious and the lips had a tendency to quiver pathetically. She fluttered down the little garden-path, looking right and left for the truants.

She discovered them bending over the great well in the garden.

"See," said little Hyacinth. "There's big cherry - tree in well, and little girl under it, also."

Aoi looked at the reflection, lingered a moment, smiling pensively at the three faces in the water, then drew them away.

"Come," she said. "Listen; those temple bells already are beginning to ring. We shall be late and disgrace his excellency."

She opened a large paper parasol, and with Koma holding her sleeve on one side and Hyacinth on the other, they

tripped up the hill to the little mission
church.

They were late, as usual, to the extreme humiliation of Aoi, who shrank
to the most obscure corner possible in
the church. She gave one anxious,
fluttering glance about her, shook her
head at the restless Hyacinth, then very
simply and naturally lifted her little,
thin voice in singing with the rest of this
strange congregation.

The old missionary at his stand, who
had seen her entrance, beamed benign-
ly upon her from over his spectacles.
Though so old, his voice could be heard
loud and clear, leading his little flock in
their hymn of invocation.

The service was exceedingly simple.
A reading from a Japanese translation
of the Bible, a few announcements by
the old pastor, then an address by a thin,
curious-looking stranger, the new assistant of the missionary. After that followed the offerings, to which every one
in the church contributed, even the chil-

49

dren, then a sweet hymn, a solemn word of benediction, and church was over.

How strangely like the church in his own home in far-away England was this little mission-house to the old minister! These gentle people had labored to erect this house on the plan he had described to them. They lifted up the same voices in melodious hymns of praise to the same Creator. Their eyes looked up to their leader with the same profound devotion. Yes, surely, he had done right in the desertion of that small pastorate in England, which a hundred ministers could fill. Here lay his true work—the fruits of his labors. This had become his home.

So down the aisle he went, followed by his new assistant—with a word and a smile, and a hearty grip of the hand for each and all of his little band.

Aoi stood in the little pew, her face turned towards him, wistfully expectant. Even the restless Hyacinth peered at him with sombre, quieted gaze.

"Ah," he said, "Mrs. Montrose and Koma. How is my little girl?" and he patted Hyacinth upon the head.

The new minister stared with some surprise at the two children, then looked questioningly at the old missionary. He was listening attentively and with old-fashioned courtesy to the words of the anxious Aoi.

"Is it not yet time, excellency? The boy is growing beyond me. What is to be done? I have taught him all the words I myself know of the English language, but, alas! I am very ignorant, and my tongue trips and halts."

The missionary glanced gravely and thoughtfully at Koma, who was engaged in whispering to the inquisitive Hyacinth. The latter was intently engrossed in regarding the pale and anæmic face of the new minister.

"He seems such a boy—such a child," said the old missionary, "I think you have done well by him, and it certainly was wise to keep him from the schools in Sendai."

"Ah, excellency," said Aoi, "he merely looks like a child. He is, indeed, much older than he appears. Was he not always old for his age? It is merely his constant association with the tiny one which causes him to appear so young."

"Well," said the missionary, "we must think about it. I will talk it over with Mr. Blount." He indicated his assistant, who bowed quietly.

Aoi appeared troubled.

"Excellency," she said, "it was the will of his august father that he should see something of the world when he should have attained to years of manhood."

The missionary nodded thoughtfully.

"I will give you my opinion to-morrow — to - morrow evening," he said. "The matter requires serious reflection."

"Thank you," she murmured, gratefully. "You are so good the gods will bless you."

Thus, even within the house of the new religion, poor Aoi let slip from her lips that almost unconscious faith in the gods of her childhood.

VII

TWILIGHT falls slowly and tenderly in Matsushima. The trees, which spread out their arms over the waters, seem but to deepen their shadows and gradually become part of the creeping silver shadow of night. For night is scarcely dark here in the summer. The noon-rays are perpetual. The stars shine with an unusual lustre. Earth reflects the light of the moon and the stars upon its shimmering waters, its deep blue fields, its blossom - decked trees. The pebbles on the shore become whiter, and the whiteness of the sands deepens the green of the pines. Night is but one long twilight, slumberous and peaceful in fair Matsushima.

When the numerous candles are light· ed in the temples on the hills, slanting

out their glimmer upon the bewilder-
ed waters, one might almost wonder
whether the stars have changed their
place and descended like spirits to render
more fairy-like this Princess of Bays.

An oddly assorted group of five people
occupied a secluded spot on the shore.
The influence of the night was upon
them as they gazed out with seeing eyes
that reflected the beauty of the scene
and the emotions that tore at their
hearts. A mother and two children—
one, whose boy soul had only begun to
open into a graver manhood, the other
a child of seven. But seven years old
was Hyacinth, yet in the child's little
face shone the restless, passionate nature
of one old enough to feel an infinity of
suffering. She it was who helplessly
sobbed as they stood there by the bay—
sobbed with an effort at strangulation,
and who gazed not alone at the magic
of the scene, but upward into the face of
Komazawa.

One of the ministers broke the painful

silence. An eager, odd, and somewhat nervous young man he appeared.

"Dear friend," he said, addressing the boy Koma, "it will be much for the best. Our good friend here agrees with me in believing that it is your duty to follow the wishes of your father."

Koma did not reply, but little Hyacinth raised a face of turbulent scorn towards the speaker. She did not speak, but contented herself with clasping the hand of Koma the tighter, pressing her face close against it.

"Possibly it might be as well to put off for a year—" began the elder missionary, hesitatingly. Aoi interrupted:

"Nay, excellency, the humble one agrees with the illustrious one. My lord's son has come to manhood. It is time now that he should leave us," her voice faltered—"for a season," she added, softly.

The Reverend Mr. Blount bowed gravely.

"I am glad, madame," he said, "to

56

find that your views coincide with mine. Your son is—er—first of all more English than Japanese."

Koma stirred uneasily. He opened his lips as though about to speak, then closed them and turned his face towards the speaker.

"He is, in fact, one of us," continued the minister. "He has the physical appearance, somewhat of the training, and, let us hope, the natural instincts of the Caucasian. It would be not only ludicrous but wicked for him to continue here in this isolated spot, where he is, may we say, an alien, and particularly when it is his duty to follow the wishes of his father as regards his English estate. Certainly this is not where Komazawa belongs."

"I do not agree with you, excellency," said Koma, with a queer accent. "This is, indeed, my home. Do not, I beg you, be deceived in that matter. It is true that I am also Engleesh, but, ah, I am not so base to deny my other blood.

57

Is it not so good, excellency? Could I
despise this land of my birth, my honorable, dear home?"

"Nay, son," interposed the agitated
Aoi, "his excellency meant no reflection
upon our Japan. But, oh, my son, you
would not rebel against the will of your
father?"

"No," said Koma, clinching his hands
at his side, "I would not."

"Then you will go to this England,
like a good son. The time has come."

Koma remained plunged in gloomy
thought.

After a moment he lifted his head and
looked at the elder missionary.

"How do we know the time has come?"

"Because, my son, you have arrived
at the years of manhood."

"I am but sixteen years."

The younger minister answered,
quickly:

"It will require four or five years, at
least, in England to learn the language
and ways of your people thoroughly."

58

"I already speak that language," said Koma, flushing darkly. "Do I not, sir excellency?"

"No and yes. You have been brought up to speak the language. It is intelligible, but queer—wrong, somehow. You speak your father's language like a foreigner."

"Very well," agreed Koma, bitterly. "Let us admit that. But may I inquire whether it will be necessary for me to go all the way to England to learn that language?"

"Well, yes. Four years in an English school will do much for you."

"Four years; and when those four years are ended I still will lack one year from my majority."

"That's right," said the missionary. "In England one attains one's majority at twenty-one. So you would have a year in which to return, if you wish it, to Japan, previous to settling in England."

"I do not know if I shall ever do that," said the boy, sadly.

"It was the wish of your father," said Aoi, pathetically.

"Yes, it was his wish," repeated Koma. "Yet I will come back each year."

"That is right," said the old minister, patting him on the shoulder.

"Your father *never* came back," said Aoi, sighing wistfully.

"It would be entirely out of the question for you to return each year. Be advised by me, Komazawa; I have your interest at heart," said the young minister, earnestly. "Stay in England four years, then return and visit your mother and sister."

"Let the good excellency decide for us," said Aoi, glancing appealingly at her old friend. He drew his brows together.

"Wait till the time comes to decide that," he concluded. "If the boy is old enough to leave home, he is of an age, also, to choose what he shall do. Let us not attempt to curb him."

60

VIII

THE new missionary assumed that Hyacinth was the sister of Komazawa. His interest in her was less than in Komazawa, since the boy was his father's heir. Possibly, too, this might have been because of the natural antagonism with which the little girl had from the first met his overtures to her. From the moment when she became acutely aware that the new minister was practically responsible for the departure of her beloved Koma, the child conceived a violent dislike for him.

When the old minister, worn with his years of labor, quietly resigned his pastorate into the hands of his successor, and the new minister had taken up the management of the little church, Hyacinth refused henceforth even to enter the mission - house. All the entreaties and threats of Aoi were in vain, and, with Koma gone, she soon realized the fruitlessness of attempting to force her to do anything against her will. Comprehending the turbulent nature of the child, she knew that Hyacinth would only disgrace them both if she were forced into the church. So the departure of Komazawa meant at least the Sunday freedom of Hyacinth.

Nor was this the only result. The child, whose strange, independent nature had never been controlled by any one save by Koma, now that he was gone broke all restraints. She wandered at will about the bay, hiding in hollows in the rocks among the tombs when they sought to find her. Her little vagabond existence was not unlike that which Koma himself had led in his early childhood, save that she was not so easily restrained by the reproaches of Aoi. Like him, at this time, she scorned the companionship of other children. Like him she wan-

dered away from her home in fits and
starts, passive for an interval, and then
bursting all bounds and disappearing
sometimes for the space of an entire day
or night, to return ragged and raven-
ously hungry.

But when the winter came, and the
snow and icicles crested the trees and
whitened the hills, poor Hyacinth was
like a little, languishing, caged bird.
Her face grew wistful and mournful.
She would remain for hours with her
face pressed against the street shoji,
staring out into the white, cold world
that bounded the horizon on all sides.
If you had asked her what she was waiting for, she would have replied:

"I am waiting for the summer, for the
summer brings Koma. He has promised."

Yet when the summer came no Koma
returned with the flowers and the sun.

Little Hyacinth grew accustomed to
her solitude. The following year she
came under the new edict of education,

compulsory everywhere in Japan, and, in spite of her protests, was forced into school with a half - score of Japanese children of her own age.

At first she regarded with a fierce detestation the school and all connected with it. Did not the sensei (teacher), on the very first day, perch his spectacles upon his nose, and, drawing her by the sleeve to one side, examine her with the curiosity he would have bestowed upon some small animal. The children eyed her askance. One or two of the larger ones pointed at her hair, and, laughing shrilly, called her a strange name. If familiarity breeds contempt it also breeds toleration with the young. Hyacinth in the beginning had merely excited the curiosity, not the antipathy, of the Japanese teacher and his scholars. But as time passed they became accustomed to the difference between her and themselves. Gradually she slipped into being regarded and treated as one of them.

Then Hyacinth's small, lonesome soul expanded to stretch out timid though passionate glad hands of comradeship to all the world. She became a favorite, the very life and soul of the school. Japanese children are painfully docile and passive. Never were such strange spirits infused into a Japanese class before.

So the years passed, not unhappily, for Hyacinth. Koma at the end of the second year was a mere memory, at the end of the third he was forgotten— wholly forgotten. Such is the fickle mind of a child of the nature of Hyacinth.

The fourth year brought him back to Matsushima. He had become very tall, taller than any of the inhabitants of Sendai he seemed, quite a head over them. He wore strange and unpleasant-looking clothes, such as those worn by the Reverend Mr. Blount, who was disliked as heartily as his predecessor had been beloved.

Koma was now an object of the greatest curiosity to Hyacinth. At first his strange appearance in the house frightened her into speechlessness. Never had she seen in all her minute experience such a strange-apparelled being, save, of course, the "abominable Blount." In concert with the small children of the neighborhood, and in spite of the remonstrances of Aoi, Hyacinth would shout strange names whenever the gaunt figure of the white missionary appeared. "Forn debbil! Clistian!"—such were the names this little Caucasian bestowed upon the representative of her race.

She had become the most utter little backslider, if she could ever have been considered a member of the church. Respect and awe for the teachings of a careful and pious Shinto teacher, and association with a score of Shinto children, had had their due effect upon Hyacinth, and the influence of Aoi waned with the years. Little if anything of the ethics of the two religions did she understand, but to her the gods were bright, beaute-

66

ous beings, whose temples were glittering gold, and whose priests kept them fragrant with incense and beaming lights by night. The mission-house was empty, ugly, dark, and damp—so it seemed to her—and an odious man, with terrible, long hairs falling from his chin, shouted and gesticulated to a congregation which often wept and groaned in unison.

The small children shouted derisively and often threw stones at the "abominable Blount" when in little groups together. But when one of their number met the minister alone, he would run from him in a sheer agony of fright.

So when Komazawa returned to Sendai, clad in the garments worn by the missionary, Hyacinth regarded him with mingled feelings of terror and fascination.

Though he made ceaseless efforts to speak to her, she could not be brought to utter one word in response. His every movement mystified her. She would sit on the floor through an entire

67

meal watching him with wide eyes while
he ate in a fashion she had never seen or
heard of before.

Koma had discarded the chop-sticks,
and now used, to the extreme joy and
agitation of Aoi, great silver knives and
forks, which she brought forth from a
mysterious recess, which even the inquisitive Hyacinth had never discovered
before.

Koma, distressed over the change in
his little playmate, sought to win her
friendship with presents purchased in
England, boxes of strange sweetmeats
—at least he told her they were sweetmeats. But they were coated with a
black-brown covering which the little
girl regarded suspiciously. She pushed
almost fearfully from her the harmless
chocolate drops. The sugar-coated bis-
cuits tempted her to touch one with the
tip of her tongue, but she retreated the
next moment when she found the red
coloring upon her fingers.

Koma regarded the girl with an expression half whimsical, half tragical, and, turning to his mother, said:

"Why, the little one is even more Japanese than I."

Aoi nodded her head, smiling tenderly at the flushing face of Hyacinth.

"Will you not even speak to Komazawa?" she inquired, reproachfully. "Why, that is not kind. Do you not love your august brother?"

As Hyacinth made no response, Koma held out his hands to her.

"Come here, little one," he said, bending to her till his face was quite close to hers.

Her fascinated eyes wandered from his strange apparel to his face. His eyes held hers with their strong, tender, reassuring expression. Half unconsciously she went closer to him.

"Do you not remember me, then?" he queried, in a soft voice, whose reproachful tones thrilled the girl.

Wistfully she approached him still closer, only to retreat in panic the next

moment.   She was like a little wild bird,
shy and fearful, yet half anxious to make
friends with a strange being.

Suddenly she began to cry, drawing
her sleeve across her eyes and turning
her face to the wall.   She could not have
told why she wept.   Was it fear, childish
conscience, or a slow recognition of her
old, beloved Koma, whose name had become but a word to her?

If she remembered Koma at all, the
memory bore no resemblance to this tall
man-boy who had returned so suddenly
to their home.   To her he seemed a
stranger, a fearful intruder.

Hurt to the quick, Madame Aoi whispered to her son.   He arose without a
word and disappeared into his room.
Fifteen minutes later, Hyacinth, playing
with a regiment of Japanese doll soldiers
on the floor, having forgotten all her
tears of a few minutes since, leaped to
her feet suddenly, with a strange, little
cry.

There in the middle of the room she

stood, holding tightly in her hand her doll, and staring, as if fascinated by the smiling figure on the threshold. It was the same stranger surely, yet, ah, not the same. A few minutes had wrought such a change in his appearance. He had discarded the heavy, dark, mysterious clothes. He appeared like any other Japanese youth, save that he was much taller, and his face smiled down upon the little girl with an expression whose power she had been unable to resist even when he had worn those outlandish garments. He called to her, softly.

"Now, come, little one; come, give me that welcome home."

Her hand unclinched, the doll dropped to the floor. With a sudden impulse she ran blindly towards him, and he caught her in his arms with a great hug, which was as familiar to her as life itself.

IX

IT was late in December, the time of Great Snow. Komazawa was still in Sendai, and Hyacinth had been taken from the school. She was now twelve years of age, still undeveloped in body and childish in mind.

Hyacinth, like most impressionable children, had quickly succumbed to the influence of the school-teacher. In his hands she had yielded like plaster to the sculptor. Out of crude, almost wild, material had been developed what seemed on the surface an admirable example of a Japanese child.

Komazawa, fresh from four years of training at an English school and intimate association with English students and professors, now set about the task of undermining all that the sensei had taught Hyacinth.

This was no light task. Hyacinth could not unlearn in a few months that which had practically become ingrained. Quite useless it was, therefore, for Komazawa to seek to turn the child's mind to a new and alien point of view, when, too, this view-point was, in a measure, an acquired thing with Koma himself. Yet he was patient, and labored unceasingly.

No; the people in the West were not all savages and barbarians.

"Did they not look like the Reverend Blount?" would inquire his small pupil.

"Yes, somewhat like him."

"Ah, then, they perhaps were not savages, but they certainly were monsters."

"No; they are very fine people—high, great."

"But only monsters and evil spirits have hair growing from the chin and awful, blue-glass eyes," protested Hyacinth.

73

Whereupon Koma quietly brought a small mirror from his room, held it before her face, and bade her look within.

She stared curiously and somewhat timorously.

"What do you see?" he inquired, quietly.

"Little girl," she said, in a faint voice.

"Yes, and what color are her eyes?"

The eyes within the glass became enlarged with excitement. The lips parted. Hyacinth put her face close to the glass.

"They are blue, also," she said, shrinking.

"Very well, then. You, also, have blue eyes, Hyacinth."

"Me!" She stared up at him, aghast.

"Certainly. Is not the little girl in the glass you?"

"No!" Her dilated eyes strained at the glass, then looked behind it and about her. She could see no other little girl in the room. There was only that

74

face in the shining glass, with its blue, shiny eyes. With spasmodic working of features, she regarded it.

"This is you — certainly," repeated Koma, pointing to the reflection.

An uncanny fear took possession of the little girl. Suddenly she raised her hand, knocking the glass from that of Koma.

"That's not me. No! That's lie. I am here—here! That's not me."

She burst into a passion of tears.

Raising the glass, Koma put it aside. He sought his mother immediately, and, with concern and perplexity in his face, told her of the incident of the mirror.

"Hyacinth was frightened—yes, actually afraid of the mirror. What can be the matter?"

"That is only natural," said Aoi. "And I am much distressed that you should have frightened her with the glass."

"But why should it affright her?"

75

"Because she has never seen one before."

"Never seen a mirror before?"

"No. It is only of late years that they have come to Sendai, my son."

"Why, the mirror is as old as the nation."

"Oh, son, but not for general use. Until recent years they were regarded as things of mystery, and were very precious and priceless."

"Yet as a child I had often seen my father's mirror. Our house contains one, does it not?"

"True; but it is locked away in our secret panel."

"But why?"

Aoi hesitated.

"It was, perhaps, a useless custom, my son. But in my younger days maidens were not permitted to see their own faces. The mirror was for the married woman only. Thus, a maiden was saved from being vain of her beauty."

Koma frowned impatiently.

"A useless and foolish custom, truly.
And now, here in these enlightened times,
you put it into practice with Hyacinth.
Why, you are prolonging the customs of
the ancients here in this house, which
should be an example of the new and
enlightened age."

Meekly Aoi bowed her head.

"You are honorably right, my son;
yet there was another reason why the
mirror was kept from the sight of the
little one."

"Yes?"

"How could I blast the little one's life
by letting her know of—of her peculiar
physical misfortunes?"

"Physical misfortunes! What do you
mean?"

"Why, the hair, eyes, skin — how
strange, how unnatural!"

Koma threw back his head and laughed with an angry note.

"Oh, my mother, you are growing
backward. You are seeing all things
from a narrowing point of view. Be-

77

cause Hyacinth is not like other Japanese children, she is not ugly. Why, the little one is beautiful, quite so, in her own way."

Aoi appeared troubled.

"You did not consider my father ugly, did you?"

"Ah no."

"Well, but was he not fair of face?"

"It is true," she admitted; then, sighing, added, "But I fear the little one would not agree with us in the matter. It might terrify her to see her own face —so different from that of her playmates. In heart and nature she is all Japanese."

"Nay; her natural parts have had no opportunities. She, like you, has seen only one side of life and the world. Now, is it not time to educate her real self?"

With an unconscious motion of distress, Aoi wrung her hands.

"The task is beyond me, my son. How can I effect it? Alas! as you say, I am in the same condition, for am I not

78

all Japanese? My lord is gone these
many years. I cannot keep step with
the passage of time. Yes, son, I slip
backward into the old mode of life and
thought. When you were by my side,
you were the prop that kept me awake,
alive. But you were gone so long. Ah!
it seemed as if time would never end."

"Oh, my mother," he cried, "I will
never leave you again. It is I who am
all wrong, wrong—I who am the rene-
gade. But we will remain here together, and you, dear mother, will teach
me all over again the precepts of my
childhood. For these four years I have
been studying, acquiring a new method
of thought and life, yet I fell into it
naturally. My father's blood was strong
in me. Yet, dear mother, now I feel I
have been wrong in leaving you, and I
will not return."

"Oh, son," she said, with trembling
lips, "you are all Engleesh — all your
father. And it is right. Do not speak
of remaining here with us. A mother's

79

eyes can see deep beyond the shallows into her child's soul. I know your restless heart cries for the other world. It is there, indeed, you belong. And you must return to this England and the college."

"But I shall not remain," he said, throwing his arm about her shoulder. "No; I shall come back when I am through college, for you and Hyacinth."

Aoi did not speak. Her poor little hands trembled against his arms.

Fluttering to the door came Hyacinth. The tear-stains were gone from her face. In her hand she carried the small English mirror. Evidently she had overcome her repugnance and fear of it, and now regarded it as some strange and active possession.

Aoi looked up at her son with questioning eyes.

"The little one's new education must commence at once," he said, slowly.

He went to the child and took the

mirror from her hand and again held it before her face.

"This is the beginning," he said. "Let her become acquainted with herself as she is. This will force a new trend of thought."

Then to the child:

"Who is this within?" he asked.

"It is I," she said, simply.

She had discovered the secret of the mirror, and somehow it had lost all terror for her—nay, it held her with a strange delight and fascination.

"Little one," said Komazawa, kneeling beside her, "look very often into the honorable mirror—every day. There you will see your own image. You will not be ignorant of yourself. You will learn much which the sensei cannot teach you. Also, go each day to the mission-house. No; do not shake your head so. But every day you must go to the school class. Then very soon, maybe in three years, I will return and complete the teaching."

Hyacinth looked timidly up into his earnest face a moment. Then she suddenly smiled and dimpled.

"Very well," she said, in English, in a tone whose note expressed as words could not her perplexed emotion.

A smile overspread Koma's face.

"Ah," he said, with a glance back at his mother, "the little one has not forgotten."

"Yet," said Aoi, "she has not spoken it, son, since you left Sendai five years ago."

X

THE Reverend Mr. Blount knocked sharply at the door of Madame Aoi's house. There was no response at first to his summons, beyond a slight stir and bustle at the rear. After a pause the sliding doors were pushed aside and the fat face of Mumè appeared for a moment, to disappear the next. She was heard chattering, in a grumbling voice, to some one within.

The visitor, grown impatient, rapped hard upon the panelling. A moment later there was the light patter of feet along the hall and Aoi appeared. She hastened towards the visitor with an apologetic expression.

Would the honorable one pardon her great discourtesy? She had been taking

her noonday siesta and had not heard the
visitor's knock. She would immediately reprove her insignificantly rude and
ignorant servant for not having shown
the illustrious one welcome and hospitality.

"I want to see Hyacinth," said the
caller, entering the guest-room and slowly removing his kid gloves.

Hyacinth, Aoi informed her visitor,
was also taking her noon sleep. Would
the honorable one deign to excuse her,
or should she disturb the little one?

"Asleep?" he repeated, disapproving-
ly. "How can that be, madame, since I
only just saw her at the window?"

"She must have awakened, then,"
said Aoi, simply.

The other nodded curtly. "No
doubt," he said. He seated himself
stiffly in the only chair in the room, and
when Aoi had quietly seated herself on
a mat some distance from him, he clasped his hands together and leaned forward towards her.

84

"Madame Aoi," he said, "I have just heard the most improbable, ridiculous tale about Hyacinth."

Madame Aoi elevated her eyes in gentle question.

"That she is, in fact—er—engaged——that is, affianced—you know what I mean."

Aoi smiled beamingly. Yes, she admitted, her daughter was, indeed, betrothed to Yamashiro Yoshida, "son of our most illustrious and respected and honorable friend in Sendai, Yamashiro Shawtaro."

"But," said the visitor, after a moment of speechless surprise, "this is the most preposterous, impossible of things. Why this — this Yamashiro Shawtaro, the father of the boy, is one of the most rabid Buddhists, and, besides, it is barbaric, an unheard - of thing, to think of marrying a girl of her age to any one."

"The betrothal," said Aoi, with a slight smile, "was all arranged by the

85

Yamashiro family. The boy is the father's salt of life. He cast eyes of desire upon the little one, and as he is the richest, noblest, and proudest youth in Sendai, we have accepted him. All the town envies us, excellency."

"Does her brother know about this?" demanded Mr. Blount, severely.

"Oh yes, surely."

"And what does he say? He is English enough to perceive the utter impossibility of such a marriage."

"We have not heard from my son yet in the matter," said Aoi, simply.

"Well," said the other, "I can assure you that when he knows the truth he will refuse to countenance it."

"But, illustrious master, how can he do so? He has not that right."

"He has not the right! Why, even your Japanese law makes him her rightful guardian. He is still a citizen of Japan. A brother, in Japan, is his sister's legal guardian. I know this to be a fact."

86

"Ah, but, honored sir, you do not know everything."

Mr. Blount looked over his gold-rimmed spectacles sharply, endeavoring to pierce beneath the softness of her tone. Japanese women were all guile was his inner comment.

"Well, now, suppose you explain to me why your son is not his sister's guardian?"

"Because, august minister, he is not the little one's actual brother."

Mr. Blount started so that he actually bounded from his seat.

"What do you mean?" he jerked out to Aoi.

"The little one is only my adopted child," said Aoi, smiling serenely.

The minister could scarcely believe he heard aright. The Japanese woman continued to smile in a manner whose guileless, impenetrable innocence of expression had the effect of irritating him excessively.

"If Hyacinth is not your child, Madame Aoi, who are her parents?"

87

"The gods forsaken little Hyacinth. She has no true parents."

In his acute interest in the matter, the minister actually overlooked the slip of Aoi when she alluded to the "gods." What he said, with his eyes fixed very sternly upon her face, was:

"You are deceiving me, Madame Aoi. You are hiding the truth from me."

The slightest frown passed over Aoi's face. Her color deepened, then faded, leaving her inscrutable and impassive once more.

The honorable one was augustly mistaken, for the humble one had nothing to hide. Since the affairs of her adopted child concerned only her foster-parent, it was impossible to deceive the honorable minister.

It was the visitor's turn to flush, and he did so angrily. Plainly this Japanese woman was attempting to conceal, with the prevarication and guile of her people, some mystery concerning Hyacinth. If the girl was not the daughter

88

of Aoi by her English husband, who then was she? She certainly was not pure Japanese. Could it be that she was not even in part Japanese? The possibility staggered the missionary.

"Madame Aoi, you are taking a most unusual attitude towards me to-day."

Aoi inclined her head in a motion that might have meant either assent or negation.

"Hitherto," continued the other, "you have not hesitated to accept my advice—"

"In matters concerning that religion, yes," interposed Aoi, softly.

"Which surely concerns all other matters connected with your welfare and that of Hyacinth. No one knows better than you do that the lives of our parishioners, our children, are our particular care and charge. I take the interest of a parent in our little band. So you would not withhold your confidence from a parent?"

"What is it the honorable sir would know?"

"The history of Hyacinth—who she is, how you came by her, her people's name—all information about her."

"There is nothing to confide," said Aoi, slowly, as though she chose her words carefully before replying. "The old excellency knew the history of the child. It was under his advice that the humble one adopted the little one."

"Under Mr. Radcliffe's advice!"

"Yes."

"What did he know of Hyacinth?"

"The excellency deigned to make effort to discover the little one's parents."

"But you don't mean to tell me that you did not know her parents?"

"Only the mother, and she lived but a day after the coming of the child."

"Did Mr. Radcliffe fail to find her father?"

Nervously Aoi clasped her hands together. She did not answer.

"Did he find her father?" repeated Mr. Blount.

Aoi looked at him with a gleam of stubbornness in her glance.

"If the excellency did not make confidant of you before he died, why should I do so, also?"

"It is your duty, madame."

She shook her head slowly.

"Certainly, it is your duty. It is perfectly plain that Hyacinth is a white— that she's not pure Japanese, at all events."

Aoi moved uneasily. Then she looked up very earnestly at her interlocutor.

"The little one knows nothing of her parentage, save that she is an orphan confided to my care. It would distress her to be told that — that she is not Japanese."

"Then you admit that?"

"No; I do not so admit. I but begged the honorable one to put no such notion into her mind, so sorely would it distress her."

"I wouldn't think of keeping her in ignorance," exclaimed the other, with some indignation. "She ought to have been told the truth long ago. I shall certainly tell her."

"What can you tell her?"

Aoi had risen and was regarding the missionary with a strange expression.

"That I suspect she is not Japanese —not all Japanese."

"She would not believe you," said Aoi, thoughtfully.

"I will see her at once, if you will allow me," said Mr. Blount, also rising. He was somewhat startled at the attitude and the reply of Aoi. She had placed herself before the door, as if to prevent the passage of any one desiring to enter.

"My daughter will not see visitors to-day," she said. "You will excuse her."

The next moment she had clapped her hands loudly. In answer to her summons, Mumè came shuffling into the room, hastily wiping her hands upon her sleeves, and looking inquiringly towards her mistress.

"The illustrious one," said Aoi, with

92

intense sweetness, "wishes to return home. Pray, conduct him to the street."

She bowed with profound grace to the missionary, and stepped aside to permit him to pass.

He hesitated a moment, and then said, slowly and succinctly:

"Madame Aoi, I have only this to say. I shall immediately take it upon myself to unravel this mystery. I will communicate with the nearest open port at once, and find out whether my predecessor had correspondence with any one on this subject. Good-day." He bowed stiffly.

XI

MEANWHILE Hyacinth lay stretched upon the matted floor of her chamber, her chin in one hand, the other holding an ancient oval mirror. She was studying her face closely, critically, and also wistfully.

The head was quaintly Japanese, yet the face was oddly at variance. For the hair was dressed in the prevailing mode of the Japanese maid of beauty and fashion in Sendai. It was a very elaborate coiffure, spread out on either side in the shape of the wings of a butterfly. Upon both sides of the little mountain at top projected long, dagger-like pins; gold they were and jewelled—the gift of Yoshida.

Hyacinth no longer fretted under the hands of a hair-dresser, since it was her

pride and delight to have her hair dressed in this becoming and striking mode.
If the hair-dresser, who came once a
fortnight, puckered her face and shook
her head when the beautiful, soft, brown
locks twisted about her fingers, and did
not follow the usual plastic methods
used upon the hair of most Japanese
maids, Hyacinth cared little. When the
operation was completed, her hair, dark,
shining, and smooth, appeared little different from that of other girls in the
village.

It was the face beneath the coiffure
that distressed the girl. The eyes were
undoubtedly gray-blue. They were large,
too, and wore an expression of wistful
questioning which had only come there,
perhaps, since the girl had begun to look
into the mirror and to discover the secret
of those strange, unnatural eyes.

The whiteness of her skin pleased her.
What girl of her acquaintance would not
be glad of such a complexion? She had
small use for the powder-pot, into which

her friends must dip so freely. Her mouth was rosy, the teeth within white and sparkling. Her chin was dimpled at the side and tipped with the same rose that dwelt in her rounded cheeks. The little nose was thin and delicate, piquant in shape and expression.

Why should such a face have distressed her? She would not admit to herself that she was homely. Perfume, Dewdrop, Spring—what did their judgment amount to? They were rude, uncouth even to have hinted at her "deformities." They were one-eyed, seeing but one type of beauty. There must be another kind, for she was surely, surely beautiful. Then she fell into a reverie in which she speculated upon the possible existence of another people whose maidens' hair and eyes were not like the night, but reflected the day.

Yet Yoshida, the son of Yamashiro Shawtaro, had actually suggested to her once, with a shamefaced expression, that if she stood in the sun-rays the goddess

96

might darken her skin and eyes! Also, he had brought her, all the way from Tokyo, a little box of oil with which to shade her hair!

The oil had disappeared in the bay, though the pretty box in which it had come had been placed with the other gifts of Yoshida. As for the sun-goddess—those at the mission-house had insisted that there was no such being. Great and wise were the mission-house people, since they had come from the land of Komazawa.

Komazawa represented to her all that was fine and great and good. He was the beloved of Aoi, and the good God had given him to her for a brother and a hero. He wrote to her every week from the other end of the world, never forgetting. His letters were the sun and light of Aoi's life, and Hyacinth shared with her something of the joy of receiving them. These two talked of him always. They watched for his letters, and devoured them with eager little

97

outcries to each other when they arrived.

He was in London. College was done for the year. He was going to Cheshire, though apprehensive of the welcome he would receive from his father's people. But the lawsuit had been won, with scarcely any struggle. His claim, his papers, withstood the closest of legal scrutiny. Yes; he was now an Englishman, almost entirely. Yet, ah, how he longed for home—for his mother and for little Hyacinth. The estate was very large, his lawyers told him, so large that he could not live there alone. Soon he was coming to take back with him the little mother and sister. Yes; it would be strange at first, but they would soon become accustomed to it. It was a cold country, and the milk of human kindness ran not freely, but it satisfied the desires of an ambitious one.

So ran his last letter.

Hyacinth wondered, vaguely, what he would say when he returned to Japan and found that she could not accompany him. By that time she would be married—married to Yamashiro Yoshida, who was rich and owned large stores in Tokyo, and who sometimes wore an English hat, the envy and marvel of all the gilded youth of Sendai.

Upon her cogitations came Aoi, trembling and anxious. She hovered a moment over the girl, hesitation and worry depicted in her countenance.

In surprise, Hyacinth looked up at her, then, carefully slipping the mirror into her sleeve, raised herself erect.

"What is troubling you, mother? Why, your hands tremble. I will hold them. You have news from Koma? What is it?"

"No, little one; it is not of Koma I speak."

"Of whom, then?"

"Of you."

"Then smile instantly. I am an insignificant subject for mirth, not tears."

"Little one, if the right of freedom

99

were given you, would you leave the humble one?"

"No; not in ten million years. What sort of freedom would that be?"

"Yet the learned ones at the mission-house will surely persuade you to take some such step."

Hyacinth laughed scornfully.

"One cannot persuade a humming-bird to come to one's hand. No; nor can these ones of the mission - house persuade me to do aught against my will."

"But they of the mission-house—Mr. Blount—insinuated that we have not the right to possess you."

"He is foolish. He has blue eyes," said she of the blue eyes, disdainfully.

"Yet it is true that we have no legal right to you," said Aoi, sadly.

"No? And why have you not?"

"Because I am not your real mother, and the time may come when others may claim you."

"Since my own mother is gone, has

not my foster - mother all right over me?"

"I do not know the law as to that," said Aoi. "Oh, if the old, good excellency were but still alive to enlighten and advise us."

"Mother," said Hyacinth, looking up with questioning, wistful eyes at Aoi, "I have never asked a question of you concerning my own mother. You were always enough for me. I needed no other parent, dear, dear one. Yet now I would ask, can you tell me aught concerning my people?"

"No, little one. The sick one gave to me no information of her people. The good excellency made effort to find them, but failed."

"My mother was a stranger to Sendai?"

"Yes, a stranger."

"And she left nothing—nothing for —me?"

Aoi hesitated a moment, then, crossing the room, slipped her hand deftly along the wall and pushed aside a small panel. Hyacinth arose slowly. Her eyes were apprehensive, her lips apart. She had grown white with expectation.

"Here, in your own chamber, little one, is all that the august one left. I would have given you them on your wedding-day."

Fearfully the girl touched the things in the little cupboard. How long had they lain there untouched? There were a woman's strange dress, white underwear, a queer, basket-shaped thing with dark feathers upon it, a pair of black Suède gloves, small shoes, and then, in a little heap, three rings — a plain gold band, one with a large diamond, another with a ruby set between two smaller diamonds. Also a little chamois-skin bag containing a little roll of green bills and some strange coin.

Upon her knees Hyacinth fell beside the little shelf, and she stretched her arms out over it, burying her face in her sleeves.

For a long time neither of the two uttered a word. When the girl raised her face, after a long interval, it was very white, and tears streamed down her cheeks. She put out a little, groping hand to Aoi.

"Oh, you were good to her, were you not—were you not?" she whisperingly cried.

Aoi could not speak.

After a time the girl arose and reverently pushed the panel into place.

"The things are Engleesh," she said, slowly. "Is it not strange?"

"Yes," said Aoi, brokenly.

Yet even then she did not tell the girl the truth. Why she had hidden this fact always from Hyacinth she could hardly have explained even to herself. She thought she had but waited for the girl to come to years of understanding. Afterwards, when the proud Yamashiro family condescended to seek alliance with her, Aoi, faintheartedly fearful lest they should refuse to permit the marriage if they knew the truth, had carefully guarded the secret even from the girl. She knew that only a few people in the little village of Matsushima had heard of the history of the girl. It was only recently that they had moved to the City of Sendai. This match with the Yamashiro family was a thing so splendid as to be regarded with awe by Aoi. It could not be possible that such a chance would ever come again to her adopted daughter.

Now she said to the girl, placing both her hands upon her shoulders:

"Promise me, then, that you will refuse to discuss this subject with the mission-house people."

"I will not even see them," said the girl, stooping to kiss the anxious face.

"For if you should do so," said Aoi, sadly, "they might persuade you to abandon us."

"Ah, no; never, mother. No one could ever do so."

"Save Yamashiro Yoshida," said Aoi, quickly.

A cloud stole for an instant over the girl's face. She sighed as she repeated, half under her breath:

"Save Yoshida—perhaps"

XII

ABOUT a fortnight later the honorable Yamashiro family condescended to pay a visit to the house of Aoi. Although they lived but a field's length away, they came in their carriages, very elegant jinrikishas, drawn by liveried runners.

The father was imperious and lordly. A man of samurai birth, he had been one of the first to take advantage of the change in government and go immediately into trade, thus placing behind him all the traditions of caste. In Tokyo he had acquired an enormous fortune. He had a partnership there in a European store. He had purchased much of the land in the region of Sendai, and the townspeople looked with some apprehensions upon his steady advance,

knowing that wherever he set his heel
the land was despoiled of beauty.

Sendai in these latter years had become quite a bustling commercial city,
and all because of Yamashiro's enter-
prise. In ten years he had altered the
little coast town's exclusive policy. Thus
the townspeople came to believe that
Sendai could no longer remain a secluded place of abode, but would become
an ugly, commercial centre, a stamping-
ground for tradespeople, and in time an
open port for the barbarians. In the
face of the dissatisfaction of his townspeople Yamashiro steadily kept to his
march of progress. Realizing that he
could never have the affection of his
neighbors, he openly tried to play the
despot over them.

A plastic little pupil was his wife, the
typical Japanese matron, who, bowing
to the will of her lord in all things,
scarcely ever spoke save to echo his
words, and who lived but for his pleasure
and comfort.

The boy Yoshida was like his father, save that he spent his restlessness upon the pleasures of youth. Having no occasion to work, and being provided with an unlimited supply of money, Yoshida frittered his way through life with the idle and rich young men of Sendai, leisurely inventing amusements for themselves, seeking and chasing every butterfly. Not a geisha of Sendai but knew the gallant Yoshida.

Then, mothlike, with a daintier and as gay a fluttering of wings as the geishas, Hyacinth had crossed his path. Aoi had moved her home about this time from the little village on the shore of the bay to the city proper. This occurred after Komazawa's English lawsuit had been settled, so that the family were now living in more affluent circumstances.

Actually abandoning his geishas, Yoshida, to the envy of the town's young belles and beauties, offered himself to the daughter of Madame Aoi, the girl whose eyes did not slant in shape, and yet which had a trick of closing half-way and then glancing out sideways. It was as if Hyacinth, with her wide eyes, had unconsciously fallen into the habit of copying nature, where all eyes about her were narrow and seemingly half closed.

On this day Yoshida and his parents brought gifts for Aoi and her daughter; gorgeous gifts they were and very costly. The girl, quite forgetful of the presence of the watchful parents of her lover, threw all her manners to the winds when she beheld the exquisite obi her father-in-law-elect had brought her from Tokyo. Out of the room she slipped, to return in the space of a few minutes, fluttering in through the sliding-doors like a bird of gay plumage, her eyes brighter, her cheeks and lips rosier than the red gold obi twisted so entrancingly about her slender waist.

Yet in her brief absence the Yama-shiro family had exchanged significant glances and commented upon her rude actions.

"Your worthy daughter, Madame Aoi," said Yamashiro, the elder, "should be placed under the care of a severe governess."

Aoi looked appealingly from the displeased face of Yamashiro to his wife. The latter sat still as an image, her small vermilion-tipped lips closely sealed together like those of a doll.

"You would not delay the marriage, excellent Yamashiro?" inquired Aoi, faintly, the match-making vanities of a mother stirring within her.

"It might be well," said Yamashiro, stiffly. Languidly the boy interposed:

"Ah, well, she will have time to learn when she has the father and mother-in-law to teach and command her."

"True," said his father, and "True" echoed his mother, stonily, scarce parting her lips to enunciate the word.

Then Hyacinth fluttered in gayly, and the light of her smile fell upon them like a shaft of sunlight, to be dissipated, a moment later, by the enshrouding mist. She paused in her tripping pilgrimage of pride across the room, glanced flurriedly at the guests, then sat down hastily beside Madame Aoi. The next moment she was as quiet and still as Madame Yamashiro herself. Her eyes were cast down, as became her age, but even when cast down they gazed in girlish pleasure on the splendor of the new sash.

"Madame Aoi," said Yamashiro, the elder, "we come to-day not upon a visit of pleasure, but for a purpose."

Madame Aoi inclined her head attentively.

"You may not, perhaps, have heard the latest news of the town. We are to have an invasion of the barbarians— Western people, in fact."

"Ah, indeed!" Aoi's eyebrows were raised in surprise. "No, I have not heard the report."

Yamashiro breathed heavily.

"Well, this matter brings us to the object of our visit. It has been brought to my knowledge that such an invasion will be sure to affect the townspeople, particularly those who have hitherto mingled with these people."

Aoi flushed faintly.

"You allude to the mission people?" she asked.

"Yes, madame."

Aoi bowed. Hyacinth elevated her head ever so slightly. She leaned forward, and her eyes, the lids downcast, were glancing upward sidewise beneath them.

"Such of our people," continued Yamashiro, "as have chosen to affiliate with the foreigners already permitted here are likely to be intimately associated with the new arrivals, especially those who have married among them."

He paused, and coughed in his hand.

"You perceive that the bad effect of such association must be felt by those of us who will not deign to give them our friendship. Therefore, madame, knowing that your honorable daughter has spent much time with these people, we desire that hereafter she shall decline all such intimacy."

Aoi bowed her head almost to the mats.

"It shall be as your excellency desires," she said.

Then, raising her head, she asked:

"When do the honorable ones come, and why do they come?"

"They may be here already," replied Yamashiro, "and the reason why they come is because some witless members of our community have advertised in the open ports the unusual beauty of Sendai as a summer resort. The foreigners come out of curiosity. It is very unpleasant."

"Yet, excellency," said the girl, with her candid gaze upon him, "were you not the pioneer in Sendai of those who induced intercourse with these barbarians?"

"The wares of Sendai," replied the other, coldly, "were placed in Tokyo for the foreigner to purchase. We did not invite the foreigner to our city."

"Sendai is not an open port," interposed Aoi, speaking so that her daughter might cease with grace. "How can the foreigners, then, invade it?"

"They have no legal rights, but their consuls, always rapacious, have power with his Imperial Majesty. They have obtained his sanction just as did these missionaries."

"Too bad," said Aoi.

Hyacinth fidgeted. After a moment, looking fully at Yoshida, she asked:

"Are their women beautiful?"

"No, abominably ugly," he returned, frowning contemptuously.

A small, roguish smile dimpled the girl's lips.

"Perhaps," said she, "I am also like unto them."

"Never!" said Yoshida, angrily.

"If you were," said his father, "you

would never be wife to a Yamashiro.
No Yamashiro would marry a white
barbarian.''

The Yamashiro family believed Hyacinth half English. This fact galled
them, but they ignored it.

Hastily, nervously, Aoi moved closer
to her daughter, laying her hand upon
the little ones in the girl's lap.

"Please, little one," she said, "bring
for the august ones the pipes and the
tobacco-bon.''

Outside the closed shoji the girl paused
and drew from her sleeve the little hand
mirror. She looked deeply into it, her
eyes wide open now.

"Perhaps," she said, "I am like unto
them. They are not abominably ugly,
if they look like me. No, for Komazawa
is also of their blood, and I—and those
clothes were Engleesh.''

XIII

Two strangers to Sendai, tall and un-
couth-appearing foreigners, came down
the main street, walking in the swift,
swinging fashion peculiar to the West-
erner, so totally unlike the shuffling
slide of the native.

They seemed both amused and irritated at the sensation they were creating, for a veritable little procession followed at their heels. Small, solemn,
and mystified Japanese boys they were
for the most part, who regarded them
with the same awesome curiosity they
would have bestowed on a wild beast.
A round-eyed, startled little boy of
twelve had followed them all the way
from the station, through which they
had entered the city. Others had quickly joined him, until gradually the follow-

ing had increased uncomfortably for the foreigners, since these astonished and curious Japanese ran sometimes ahead of them, to stand in their track and gaze up at their faces.

Annoyed, the strangers quickened their speed to a rapid gait, which forced the sandal-wearers into a run in order to keep pace with them.

It was noonday and very warm. No jinrikishas were in sight. The strangers would have welcomed the piping cries of the numerous jinrikisha men of Tokyo, who had pestered and swarmed about them there like flies. Here in the City of Sendai there appeared to be no public jinrikisha stand as yet, and the "tavern" to which they had been directed had not as yet dawned upon their vision.

"We seem to be on the chief street," said one of them. "Better turn here."

They turned swiftly down a cross-street which seemed rather a long road, on the sides of which tall bamboos sprang upward to a great height, bend-

ing at the top into an arch which cast
its shade below. The houses were set
back some distance from the road,
though garden walls, in which were small
bamboo gates, isolated each dwelling.

The foreigners had now slackened their
speed. Their following had diminished
considerably, and those who remained
were now keeping at a respectful distance from the heavy cane which one
of the two swung back and forth in
his hand with apparent carelessness.
There was a hideous head on the knob
of this stick. Was it possible that this
might be a fiend whose touch would
kill any little boy venturing too near?
So the strangers, less troubled by their
dwindled following, began to look about
them with some interest.

The street upon which they found
themselves appeared cool and refreshing
because of its shadowing trees. There
was an atmosphere of refinement and
æstheticism about it that delighted the
appreciative foreigners.

"Do you see where it leads?" said the one of the cane, pointing with his stick down the thoroughfare.

"Straight down to the water. What a wonderful sight!"

At a point where the street curved upward to a slight elevation, Matsushima, still at a good distance from them, burst upon their view. The visitors stood as if entranced. One of them lifted a pair of field-glasses to his eyes. After a full minute's use of the glasses, he passed them silently to his companion. The other regarded the scene with equal admiration.

"We must go up there to-morrow without fail," he said, waving his hand towards the heights on the opposite shore.

"Yes," assented the other; "I understand there's quite a party coming along to-morrow."

"Yes, some Tokyo priest is escorting them. Well, a tourist might well visit. the cemetery of his household."

The other regarded him with some bewilderment.

"The cemetery of his household?" he repeated.

"This is the place where, three hundred years ago, a Japanese feudal lord, named Date, I believe, sent an envoy to Rome acknowledging the Catholic supremacy. This is practically the birthplace of Catholicism in Japan."

"Well, this is all very interesting, I must say. Yet I understand the only mission here, at present, is Presbyterian."

"Exactly. Catholicism has been practically stamped out. There was a horrible massacre of the Jesuits here at one time, I believe. This visit by the priest and the party may do something for the place."

They resumed their walk in silence.

"I don't fancy," said the elder one, "that it will be possible for us to shake off this little herd behind us. The thing for us to do is to find that will-o'-the-wisp

of a tavern or the mission-house. Where
do you suppose the place is?"

"The mission-house, rest assured, is
elevated on some hill. Suppose we turn
upward and—"

He broke off, at the same time stopping abruptly in his walk.

They were before a little garden com-
posed of white stones and fantastic-
spreading trees, seeming to bend their
boughs over the miniature lake as if to
regard their own reflected beauty. But
it was not the distinction of the garden which attracted and startled the
strangers, but the little figure which
leaned over the gate.

Filtering through the tree-top by the
gate, the sun slanted full upon the head
of the girlish form, bronzing the hair
almost to the color of deep gold. The
girl's eyes were wide open as if with faint
surprise, her lips were apart, and she
was plainly flushed with some unwonted
excitement. She wore a plum-colored
kimono, simple and exquisite. About

her waist was an old-gold obi, and there was a flower ornament in her hair. The wings of her sleeves fell backward, disclosing arms of perfect whiteness and little hands which clung in tremulous excitement to the bamboo railing of the gate.

The tourists had been some months in Japan. One of them was an attaché to an American consulate. Well acquainted as they were with the soft-eyed, cherry-lipped beauty of young Japanese girls, they stood speechless, startled, before the picture that Hyacinth presented, as she in her turn gazed in wide-eyed astonishment at them. The mission-house folk were the only Westerners she had ever seen. These strangers did not at all resemble the Reverend Blount or his friends who came at different times to visit him. Even their clothes had a different cut, and their pleasant faces, in spite of their light eyes, to which she could never become accustomed, were shaven smooth and clean.

No devils, thought Hyacinth quickly, would have such countenances. A mistake had been made in the popular impression. Nevertheless, the strangers were certainly odd curiosities.

She blushed all rosy red, even her little ears and neck tingling with pink, as they paused before her. Half unconsciously she bent her head and made a timid little motion of greeting to them.

The younger man, the one with the huge stick, said, in an undertone, "I'm going to speak to her," and he went a pace nearer.

"Can you tell me where the Dewdrop Tavern is?" he asked, in atrocious Japanese.

For a moment she hesitated. Then the faintest smile lurked at the corners of her mouth and a dimple peeped out in her chin. Her voice was sweet and low.

"The humble one cannot understand such language," she said, pretending ignorance of his words, and secretly hoping

123

that she might provoke further speech from these strange men.

Before the stranger could frame his question in plainer language, Aoi appeared in the path, hastening down anxiously to the gate. She was overwhelmed with distress, she declared, that the august ones were followed so rudely by the children of the community. Would not the excellencies condescend to pardon the little ones? They must appreciate how strange they appeared to them. But as for her, Madame Aoi, she was well acquainted with their people, since her own lord had been English also.

The two men looked at each other and then at the young girl, as though understanding now her strange beauty.

"What," asked Aoi, "is it the excellencies desire that they have deigned to halt before our insignificant abode?"

"We wish to be directed to some tavern—some place where we can secure accommodation."

124

"Ah, yes, exactly. In the village on the shore of Matsushima there is the Dewdrop Tavern, but that is some distance away. If the excellencies will follow the street for a little while longer they will come to the Snowdrop Hostelry. There the honorable ones would be welcomed with august hospitality."

The strangers lingered a moment, watching the two figures at the gate, now courtesying very deeply. Then they turned slowly and resumed their walk.

Hyacinth turned to Aoi in great excitement.

"I am going to follow them also, mother. I wish to hear them speak again. What strange, deep voices! It was enough to make a maiden jump ten feet with fright. And *how* the gods have blasted their countenances! Did you notice, mother, how their skins were bleached like white linen?"

She shuddered.

Aoi smiled indulgently.

"When one becomes accustomed to

the white skin, little one, it appears very beautiful."

"Ah, not on a man!" said the girl, with immeasurable disgust. "But perhaps it is a custom of their country. Who knows! They are barbarians, are they not? Perhaps these men whiten or chalk their skins like the priestesses at the temple."

"Nay, it is all natural."

But Hyacinth shook her head, still uncertain. Such beings were unnatural, more so even than the Reverend Blount or the mission men. Curiosity stirred within her. She must know if the strangers acted as the human beings she knew. Quickly she formed a plan. She would follow them at a distance and slip in at the back entrance of the Snowdrop Hostelry. Then surely her friend, Miss Perfume, the daughter of the proprietor of the tavern, would permit her to listen behind the shoji, and to watch these curious strangers, unperceived, through peep-holes in the wall.

XIV

THE Snowdrop Hostelry was as quaint
and refreshing as its name Here the
low - voiced, shy - faced mistress overwhelmed the strangers with expressions
of welcome, while her maidens vied with
one another in caring for their comfort.

The strangers were accustomed to the
eccentricities of the country, and so with
resignation they seated themselves upon
the floor, where on little, brightly polished lacquer trays the waiting-maids set
out for them an inviting and delightful
repast. Upon one tray was fresh and
fragrant tea; egg, fish, rice, and soup on
another; fruit—persimmons and plums
—on a third; and on a fourth slender,
long-stemmed pipes and huge tobacco-
bons.

"Now," said the younger of the two,

"we can talk with some degree of comfort and privacy."

At his companion's slight glance of uneasiness towards the waiting-maids, the other assured him they could not understand English.

"Let us go over the entire matter from the beginning, then," said the other man. "Mr. Matheson, our consul, assured me that you would give me all the assistance and information you could."

"Oh, certainly; but you must remember, Mr. Knowles, that I am entirely in ignorance as to what information you desire. Mr. Matheson gave me a number of papers in the Lorrimer affair, and I presume this case is in some way connected with yours."

"Exactly. I am Mr. Lorrimer's attorney, and have been four months in Japan looking up this matter."

"Yes?"

"You already know the circumstances?"

"No, not at all. Except that a letter

128

from some missionary started **Mr.** Matheson on an investigation which brought to light a letter written about seventeen years ago to the Nagasaki consul. He was an awful fool—the consul, you know—let everything take care of itself; so this matter was clean forgotten, or rather ignored. It seems his successor was a brighter fellow, and he sent the correspondence from Sendai to Nagasaki on to Tokyo."

"Yes, and I believe the letters you hold will supply the missing links. Let me tell you the facts of the case—that is, so far as I know them. About eighteen years ago, Mr. Lorrimer was married to a Miss Barbara Woodward, a Boston girl. The marriage was one of those unfortunate, hasty, society affairs in which the parents play the leading parts."

"I understand," the other nodded.

"They were mismated," continued the narrator—"unsuited to each other in every way. Their temperaments constantly jarred; they had few interests in common. Life became a burden to them. Time, however, did much to heal the breach, and finally Mrs. Lorrimer expected to become a mother. They were in Japan at the time, and she had a fancy that the child should be born here. In spite of her happy expectations, she became excessively morbid and pessimistic. She began to have hallucinations, to suspect my client of impossible things—infidelity and so forth —and hence acted as only a thoroughly unreasonable woman would. She conceived an unreasoning dislike for a Miss Farrell, and, I understand, accused her husband of being in love with the lady. Doubtless, fancying she was wronged, the poor, misguided thing left her husband — in short, ran away from him. Mr. Lorrimer took steps to ascertain her whereabouts, but was unsuccessful. Under the circumstances he returned to Boston, secured a divorce, and—ah— married Miss Farrell.''

The younger man frowned and cleared his throat slightly.

"Ugly affair," he simply essayed, quietly.

"Yes, it was. Average woman a fool. But now I come to my point. There was a child."

The young man whistled softly.

"I see. And the father wants it?"

"Naturally."

"And the law gives it to him?"

"Certainly. But we have reason, fortunately, to believe that in this case the power of the law will not be necessary. The mother, we believe, is dead."

"Ah!"

"Now I come to the papers in your hand."

"Oh yes; here they are. I haven't even looked at them."

"Ah!" The sheet trembled in the lawyer's hand. Adjusting his glasses, he read the paper carefully, and then struck it sharply with his hand.

"This is exactly what we want," he said; "it is enough in itself."

"Yes," said the other, laconically.

"It gives us the subsequent history of the wife and practically the whereabouts of the child at that time. Good!"

"I can't see why it is necessary for me to come. It's devilish hot," said the other, mopping his brow complainingly.

"My good fellow, you are lent to me by our consul. I believe you can assist me in the work of finding the child. It—she—is here—in Sendai, it seems—or she was. Let's see what the other missionary writes."

He unfolded the letter and read:

"*American Consul, Tokyo:*

"I take the liberty of addressing this letter to the various English, American, and German consuls in Japan. I wish to advise you that there is a white child in Sendai, the adopted daughter of a Japanese woman, concerning whose parentage there appears to be some mystery. The child has been brought up entirely as a Japanese girl, and does not know as yet of her true nationality. She is soon to be married to a Japanese youth, a Buddhist by religion. As she is a minor, and I consider this an outrage, I am of the opinion that steps should be taken to ascertain the parentage of this young white girl.

"I am, with respect,

"(Rev.) JAMES BLOUNT."

"Whew!" said the younger man. "We must be hot on the girl's trail. It would be a coincidence, wouldn't it, though, if she proved to be the same."

"The former missionary also wrote from Sendai," said the lawyer. "There is not the smallest doubt in my mind that the child is the same."

There was a slight stir behind the paper shoji beside them, causing the two men to glance towards it quickly. Then, with slight frowns, they nodded comprehendingly to each other.

"One of the unpleasant things of this country," said the younger man, "is that privacy is an unknown quantity. As you perceive, we have had not only watchers but auditors."

He indicated with a nod of his head a few little holes in the shoji, through one of which a little rosy-tipped finger protruded, as it carefully and cautiously widened the opening. The next moment the finger withdrew, and an eye, withdrawn from a smaller hole above, was applied to the larger hole. And the eye was blue!

"Christmas!" cried the attorney, springing to his feet indignantly. "Our listeners are not merely Japanese, it seems."

In vexation he strode to the shoji, shook it angrily, and then savagely pushed it aside.

There was a great fluttering from within. The sliding-doors were now pushed wide apart, showing the inner apartment in its entirety. A bright-hued kimono was disappearing around an angle which led to a long hall, and close upon its heels a girl in a plum-colored kimono tripped and fell to the floor in a heap. Over to her strode the

134

two men. She put her head to the mats
and crouched in speechless fear and
shame.

"What do you want?" the elder one
demanded; "and what do you mean by
listening at the door like this?"

She spoke with her head still bent to
the floor.

"The insignificant one wished only to
listen to the voices of the excellencies."

The peculiar quality of her voice
struck the men with a familiar tone.
It was a voice they had heard but a little time since—but where?

"But some white — somebody with
blue eyes was here, too—somebody not
Japanese."

"Excellency is augustly mistaken."

Excellency was not augustly mistaken,
and if she did not explain immediately,
excellency said he would raise the roof.

Whereat she got to her feet very
slowly, and lifted her face in strangely
tremulous appeal to them. They recognized her instantly.

"Those abominable blue eyes," she said, "alas, belong unto me." She bowed in humble deprecation.

"What were you doing?"

"Pray, pardon the foolish one. I did follow you to gaze upon you," she said.

Flattered against their will, and fascinated by the girl's peculiar beauty, the men smiled upon her.

"And why did you wish to *gaze* upon us?"

"Because, excellencies, the humble one wanted to satisfy herself whether the illustrious ones were gods — or — or—"

She retreated from them ever so slightly.

"—or," the younger man repeated— "or what?"

"Devils," she said, in a whisper.

They burst into laughter. All their good-nature was restored in a moment.

"And what are we?" inquired the elder man.

"Neither," she said, looking at their

136

faces very earnestly. "You only just plain men—just like me—same thing."

"How is it you could not understand our Japanese before, yet you answer us now?"

"My ears were stupid then. They are brighter now," was her paradoxical response.

The elder man turned to the other.

"I've an idea; let's question her. She's a half-caste, apparently, and may be able to help us in the search for the Lorrimer child."

"Good idea."

"Give me the first letter. Better make sure of the woman's name. Ah, here it is—Madame A—peculiar, unpronounceable name."

"'Hollyhock' in English," said the younger, looking over his shoulder.

The girl suddenly turned to the strangers.

"Excellencies, I also understand liddle bit Engleesh," she said.

"You do?"

"Yes. And I also listen to that conversation."

"Which was a very wrong thing to do"

She seemed serious and regarded them with an appealing expression in her eyes.

"Is there really liddle Engleesh girl at Sendai?"

"Yes. Do you know her?"

She shook her head.

"But," she said, "I extremely sorry for her."

"Why?"

"Soach a wicked fadder!"

"Oh no. He's a very fine man."

She continued to shake her head.

"He's got nudder wife now?" she suddenly asked.

"Yes."

"Then he don' also wan' his liddle girl?"

"Oh, but he does. He has no other children and is crazy to find this one."

Hyacinth sighed.

138

"Well, I think I go home. Excellencies will pardon me."

"One minute. Do you know somebody—a woman—named—how in the deuce is this pronounced, Madame A—o—"

"Madame A-o," she repeated, softly. "No, I do not know such name—but —but—my mother, her august name is liddle like that—Madame A-o-i."

The two men started, the same idea occurring in a flash to each.

"Jove!" said the younger, "our search is ended."

The girl stared at them with puzzled eyes. The elder man went a step nearer to her, bent down, and looked very closely at her face.

"Do you know," he said, slowly, "I have a strong suspicion that you—*you* are the child we are looking for?"

"Me!" she stammered.

With sudden fright her lips parted. She became snow-white, the color ebbing out from her face under their very eyes.

Her little hand was placed almost unconsciously over her heart.

"Me!" she repeated, faintly, "that —that liddle Engleesh child! Excellencies make august mistake. You excuse yourselves, if you please! You—"

Trembling she turned from them and moved towards the exit rear. As they followed her she turned her head, looking back at them over her shoulder, fright in her eyes.

Suddenly she made a quick dash forward and plunged blindly into the dark inner corridor. Her footfalls were so light they scarce could hear them, even with their ears strained, but, hastening to the window, they saw her fleeing up the street.

XV

HYACINTH did not slacken her pace until she was before her home. Then, with trembling fingers, she undid the gate, sped up the little adobe path, and burst breathlessly into the guest-chamber, where Aoi was quietly and pensively arranging blossoms in a vase.

Aoi turned with mild surprise at the girl's entry, but when she saw her face the mother hastened towards her.

"Why, something has affrighted the little one. Aré moshi, moshi. Well, she should not have followed the strangers. There, tell it all to the mother."

She drew the trembling girl to the soft-padded floor and placed her arm reassuringly about her. But Hyacinth seized both her foster-mother's hands and held them in a spasmodic, almost fierce, clasp.

"They going to come for me! Oh yes, yes. They will take me away. Oh, what can I do? What— They tell me— Oh-h—"

She broke down utterly, her throat choked with her sobs.

"Why, what does the little one mean?"

She could not respond. She clung to Aoi fearfully.

There were heavy, quick steps coming up the garden-path. Then a pause before the door. The next moment loud raps.

The young girl's trembling fear communicated itself to Aoi, and the two now clung together fearfully, listening, with strained ears, to every sound. They heard the shuffling sound of Mumè's feet in the hall, then the gruff, deep voices of the callers, and a few moments later the men were ushered into the guest-chamber of Madame Aoi.

Their mission was soon explained. They understood that seventeen years ago an American lady had died in her home, which was then in a village on the shore of the bay. She, Madame Aoi, they understood, had adopted the child, having failed to find the father. He, on his part, had only just succeeded in tracing the child's whereabouts. It was believed that she, Madame Aoi, was still in possession of her.

Although Aoi made no denial, she made no admission. She looked at the girl she had brought up as her own child with dry eyes and quivering lips. The young girl looked back at her with piteous, imploring eyes. Aoi closed her lips and refused even to answer the strangers. But after a space the girl herself stepped towards them and, raising her face defiantly, said:

"Foreigners, you make ridiculous mistake. Yet, supposing you do not make mistake, what will you do?"

"Send immediately for the father."

"And then?"

"He is your legal and natural guardian. You, of course, would have to go with him."

The lawyer did not hesitate to pronounce her the one for whom they had sought.

"Leave — Japan?" she asked, her bosom heaving.

"You are not Japanese. You see, I take it for granted you are the girl in question."

"Yes," she said, "I am that girl in question. My mother's clothes—they are Engleesh. Excellencies do not make mistake. I—I—foolish to deny that. But — but what *he* — that father going to do—*if* I will not go with him?"

"You are under age," said the lawyer. "He can force you."

"Force me to leave my home?" she said, softly. "Force me to leave Japan? No!"

"You belong to his home. It is some

144

fatal and horrible miscarriage of fate that has cast your destiny among this alien people."

"Not alien!" she said, fiercely. "*My* people—my—" She broke off, and almost staggered towards Aoi, against whom she leaned, as if for support.

"Go away, go!" she cried to them. "Excuse our rudeness, but—but, alas, we are in sorrow."

She sank to the ground, burying her face and sobbing piteously.

Aoi stepped falteringly towards them.

"Good-bye, excellencies. Pray you come to-morrow instead. We will be in good health then. Good-bye."

Silently the two men left the house. They were quite far down the street before either spoke again. Then:

"Good Heavens! It is grotesque, impossible, horrible," said the younger man.

"She is more Japanese than anything else."

"But her face—it—by George! I haven't words to express myself. I thought to render a splendid service to the little girl, yet now—well—I feel like a—criminal."

XVI

AFTER the departure of the strangers, Aoi and Hyacinth, clinging to each other, had gone to the young girl's chamber, where they had shut themselves in alone. The suddenness of the blow had robbed them of the power of even talking it over. The tension of the strain might have been relieved had they done so. But they sat in silence together throughout the night. Aoi appeared to be dazed, stunned, while the feelings of the girl were mixed. The phantoms of her ever-active mind were tangled, but painful. She was to be torn by force from her home—to be taken away from all she loved—she would never see Aoi again—Aoi, her mother, whom she loved deeply, devotedly.

She would be carried away to a

country where the people lived like barbarians and beasts—a country barren of beauty—cold, cruel. All this the misguided sensei had told her more than once. She felt sure she would languish and become mortally sick there, if she ever reached that distant country. But how would she cross the great, horrible ocean that lay between? Yes, she was quite sure she would die before she reached that America; and she did not want to die. Life had been very sweet for her, and she was so young.

Slow tears of self-pity slipped from her eyes and dropped upon her little, clasped hands. She looked across at the immovable figure of Aoi sitting in the dusky room before her like a statue. She wondered vaguely what Aoi was thinking about. How she did love that dear, small mother. She moved a pace closer to her. Aoi parted her lips as if to speak, then closed them, as though words failed her. Hyacinth covered her face with her hands.

How long they sat thus together she could not have told. Her thoughts had become blurred and distant.

Later, when Aoi roused herself from her own painful self-communings, she perceived that the young girl had fallen asleep. Her little head rested uncertainly against the wall-panelling, and Aoi saw the undried tears still upon the white, childish face. She gently placed a pillow beneath the girl's head, and softly threw over her the slumber-robe. Then she extinguished the one andon which had dimly lighted the room. She did not, however, retire to her own chamber that night, but lay down beside the girl, creeping under the same robe which covered her.

The following morning brought one of the unwelcome strangers again to the house of Madame Aoi. He was the younger one of the two, and had stood by silently while his companion explained the motive of their call.

Mumè had seen him lingering and

149

hesitating at the gate of the garden for
some time before he suddenly pushed
it open and walked a few paces swiftly
up the path, paused in thought a moment, and then continued to the house.
He had evidently expected at least a
polite reception, and was much discon-
certed when the scowling face of the
now hostile Mumè confronted him at the
threshold. This Oriental virago deigned
at first no word of question as to the
desire of the caller, but when he had
stammeringly stated in uncertain Japanese that the object of his visit was to see
Madame Aoi, she broke out into vigor-
ous and violent Japanese abuse.

What did this devil of a barbarian
want? How dared he soil the threshold
of her august mistress's house. All the
fiends of Hades were pestering them
lately, it seemed, but she, Mumè, was not
to be frightened by any such fiends as
he. He had scared the little one and her
mother quite speechless. She, Mumè,
would defend them from further violence

at his hands, and he had better begone
at once, or she would set the whole community upon him and have him stoned
and beaten.

In the midst of this harangue she
was interrupted by the interposition of
Hyacinth, who had arrived upon the
scene and had stood silently in the
background for some time quietly listening to the fluent Mumè. Then she
stepped forward and spoke a few, low
words in Japanese to Mumè. The young
man could not have told from the expression of her face whether she had
reproved the servant or not. When the
angry Mumè, muttering and scowling
at every retreating step, had disappeared, the girl turned questioningly to the
caller. She did not invite him to enter,
and though her words were courteous,
he thought her eyes antagonistic. He
noticed, too, that there were shadows
beneath the eyes, and that she was very
pale. As he continued to gaze at her
face she slowly and unwillingly flushed.

"Your business, honorable sir; what is it you desire?"

"You'll excuse me, I'm sure, but I came over—er—I came over by request of Mr. Knowles. You remember Mr. Knowles?"

He paused to gain time, still hoping she would bid him enter. But the expression of her face was coldly forbidding, and at his question she merely inclined her head with the faintest, most frigid smile on her lips. It seemed to the anxious young man that she must see through his flimsy ruse. As a matter of fact, all she thought was that here again was that odious stranger. Were the gods going to pester her forever with their company? The thought nauseated and embittered her.

"You see—Miss—er—if you will allow me a moment of your time," the young man stammered, "I can easily explain."

Again she inclined her head without speaking, as though she conceded the

152

moment of time, but had no intention
that it should be granted anywhere else.
He marvelled that the deliciously blush-
ing and ingenuously coquettish girl of
the previous day could have changed to
this cold and impassive little stiff figure
with the dignity of a woman.

"Mr. Knowles, you see, being a great
friend of your father—and mine—we
naturally feel that—er—we both wish
to express our—our—respects for his
daughter."

"Thangs," she said, laconically.

"And if you would do me the honor,"
he added, taking courage from the one
word she had allowed herself, "we would
like very much to have you and—of
course—your—Madame—A-ah—" he
floundered, hopelessly.

"Madame Aoi," said the girl, distantly.

He could not have told how he had
happened to invite them to dinner. Certainly it wouldn't do to have them come
at once. There was the attorney to be
considered—Mr. Knowles—who knew

nothing of his visit, and might, after all, disapprove of it.

"We'll send you word just when to come," he concluded, lamely.

He saw her lip curl disdainfully, and guessed aright that she was thinking him atrociously uncouth and rude in delivering so ambiguous an invitation. She said:

"We are ten million times grateful—but we don' can come—"

She paused ominously a moment, then slightly moving backward into the hall, she said:

"That's all your business—yes?"

"Yes," he said, confounded.

She closed the sliding-doors between and left him standing there facing it without.

XVII

MELANCHOLY now took up its morbid abode in the house of Madame Aoi. Even Mumè felt the pall of its heavy weight, and went about her work no longer complaining loudly, but muttering to herself — shuddering at the silence and shadow that had fallen upon the house. For Aoi, to keep out unwelcome callers, kept the shutters and shoji closed at all times, and the house assumed the aspect of one wherein was illness or sorrow.

But Hyacinth sought solace among her flowers. She kept sedulously to the back of the house, where she knew she would be safe from intrusion. Along the little, white-pebbled paths, which she and Aoi had so cunningly planned among the flower-beds, between the twisted and fantastic trees affected by

Japanese - garden lovers, she aimlessly
wandered.

Meanwhile, the young American attaché fairly haunted the vicinity of
Madame Aoi's house. He would spend
sometimes an entire morning strolling
up and down the street before the house.
Indeed, so familiar had his figure become to the neighborhood children that
he no longer was molested by them.
He had told Mr. Knowles that he was
enchanted by the view of the bay
Matsushima, but since it was too ener-
vating to walk in the heat such a distance, he preferred watching it afar
from the Pinetree Street, whence he obtained the best view possible. The
attorney, deep in the preparation of a
report and opinion to follow his cable to
Mr. Lorrimer, had merely looked up at
him keenly a moment, and, marking
the ingenuous coloring that flooded the
face of the boy, stuck his tongue in his
cheek and softly winked. Mr. Knowles
was very well satisfied, since young

Saunders would cease to complain against his enforced stay in this little inland town, so far away from the gay metropolis.

For a week Saunders patiently waited and watched for a glimpse of Hyacinth. But though, in his repeated pilgrimages up and down the street, his pace fell to almost a crawl when he would pass her home, and though he did not, after the first day, hesitate to crane his neck eagerly, and try to see beyond the bushes and trees in the front garden to the portion behind, no glimpse, as yet, had he obtained of the object of his desire. The house, indeed, seemed closed, and but for the fact that once or twice he had seen the fat form of Mumè issue forth on apparent shopping errands, he would have thought the house deserted. Once he had attempted to speak to Mumè, but she had indignantly opened an aggressive parasol squarely in his face, the points of which he had barely escaped.

Saunders became desperate. He told

himself that he had no intention whatever of allowing a fat little servant to stand in his way, nor was he to be abashed by the haughty dignity of one so completely bewitching as was this little Hyacinth.

Hence, one morning in June, Mr. Saunders came down the Pinetree Street with a much swifter and more dogged step than usual. Reaching Madame Aoi's house, he did not even linger, but, pushing the gate aside, intrepidly entered the hostile country. He was cautious, however, and, mindful of his previous visit, he turned aside from the path which led to the front threshold, and made his way softly around the side of the house. His bravery was usually short-lived, and, though possibly he would not have admitted it, his heart was thumping, and he bore the aspect of a thief, as, creeping stealthily in the shadow of the trees, he plunged ahead. He had had a purpose in mind when he started—the brave one of penetrating the back of the house.

Experience had taught him that the Japanese practically lived in this part of their house, and that the garden, unseen from the front, was where they were likely to be found. Yet he had the natural contempt of the Japanese idea of privacy. He could not accept the fact that in most personal matters of life they appeared to be almost ignorant of the word privacy.

His surmises were correct. He came upon a member of the family almost as soon as he reached the back garden. Hyacinth was sitting on the moss-grown shelf of an old well and looking at the reflection of her face listlessly, perhaps unseeingly, in the dark water beneath. She made a pretty picture, as, startled by the sudden appearance of the young man, she slipped to the ground and faced him. Her eyes were wide, half with fright, half with growing anger, and from being pale she flushed vividly red. Her voice was harsh and strained when, after a moment, she spoke.

"What do you want?"

This time she did not even give him the title of "honorable sir."

"I wanted to see you," he said, truthfully.

"You come like a thief," she said. "Is that the custom of the barbarian?"

"I beg your pardon, but really—the fact is—I hoped this way to avoid an encounter with your servant."

She made a scornful movement towards the house, but he sprang before her and barred her passage.

"See here—Miss Lorrimer—I hope you will listen to me. I know I seem to have acted atrociously, but really—"

"Have you some business to speak to my honorable mother?" she inquired, boldly.

"No—I confess I have not—but I wanted—to become acquainted with you."

After that an uncomfortable pause ensued. The girl appeared to be turning the matter over in her mind. Then she said:

"Why do you wish make acquaintance with me?"

Simple as her question was, it appeared to have glowing possibilities to the eager Saunders.

"Because," he said, "you are so lovely. Do you know—"

She interrupted him.

"Is that the manner in which your country people address maidens?" she asked, with more curiosity than offence.

"Yes—that is, sometimes—when they mean it, and the girl *is* lovely, as you are."

"But," she said, "it is augustly rude to tell me so."

"Oh no; you wouldn't think so if you understood."

"I understand," she said.

"I mean, if you understood our point of view."

"Understand it," she repeated, "but I despise it." Then, after a slight pause,

161

very earnestly: "I am a Japanese; we
are not so uncouth and rude in our intercourse with strangers."

"I wish you would not regard me as a
stranger."

She looked puzzled.

"Not regard you as a stranger!" she
repeated.

"No. I wish you'd look upon me as a
friend; one who admires you and wants
to—to do something for you."

"But you are not my friend," she
said. Then, catching her breath a moment, she added, "You are an enemy."

"I!" He was very much pained. *He*
an enemy to this charming young girl!

"Yes, yes," she said, with some ve-
hemence. "You come here into our
peaceful home and in one day — one
minute—you break it all up, bring distress and pain upon us. You have no
fine sense; you cannot even be insulted.
You come again, again, perhaps again,
though your presence we do not desire—"

162

She stopped short suddenly; her underlip quivered, and she bit it nervously with little, white teeth. She turned her back half towards young Saunders, and he could see from her trembling that she was on the verge of tears. He could only falter very earnestly:

"I am very sorry—very sorry."

She did not speak again, and for some time they stood in silence, she with her head drooping away from him and he watching her eagerly. He knew she was waiting for him to go, and he was waiting for her to turn to him again. He wanted to see her eyes, those eyes which had flashed at him so wrathfully and then had become so suddenly misty and piteous.

"Will you not at least tell me," he said, "that you will pardon—forgive me for—for my intrusion—"

"I am very unhappy," she said, still with her face turned from him. "I am not in condition to see any one—friends —strangers—any one. You have made

163

me so miserable I—I pray to the gods sometimes that I might die."

She slipped to the ground and buried her face in her arms on the little stone shelf of the well.

Now, the young attaché was really a good-hearted boy, in spite of his frivolity; and the sight of the little, sobbing figure touched him. He stood in a confusion of discomfort and remorse, while strange little waves and thrills of tender emotion swept over him and rendered him still more helpless.

He was too stupid to comprehend the cause of the girl's wretchedness, and he was very young. Consequently, he actually experienced a thrill of vague pleasure at the thought that in some way his attractive personality was responsible for Hyacinth's distress.

But while he stood hesitating and perspiring from sheer excitement, he became suddenly conscious of the fact that some one was coming from the house towards them. Aoi came hurriedly across the grass. She paused a moment, startled at the sight of the young foreigner in their private gardens. Then she saw the crouching girl, and in a moment comprehended the situation.

Poor, simple, amiable Aoi! Possibly never in all her life before had such violent feelings assailed her. She turned upon the intruder with flashing eyes.

"You come here! You make my daughter weep! You are bad lot. Leave my grounds or I will have you arrested!"

"Madame Aoi," he protested, "I assure you that I meant no offence, but—"

Hyacinth had slowly risen to her feet. She put her arm gently about Aoi's shoulder.

"Do not speak the words to him, mother," she said, in Japanese. "He did not mean to make me weep."

Aoi was quieted in an instant. She still looked uncertainly, however, at the stranger.

A sudden idea seemed to come to her

165

mind.   She went a hesitating step nearer to Saunders and raised her face to his,
while her eyes searched his face.   She
said:

"You come to see *me*, august sir, or
—or—my daughter?"

"Your—that is—"

He flushed uncomfortably, but indicated, with a slight nod of his head, the
young girl.

Aoi's eyes narrowed curiously.   Her
trembling lips compressed themselves
into a stiff, rigid line.   When she spoke
her voice was quite hoarse.

"In Japan," she said, "a young man
does not visit a maiden unless he is her
lover."

Saunders swung his stick uneasily.

"I am an American," he said, lamely.

"Yes," said Aoi.   "You are American,
and because that is so your visit to my
daughter is an insult."

"No, I protest," he said, warmly.

"You came for business?"

"No—but—"

166

"You came to make that love to her
—yes—it is so?"

"Yes—but—er—"

Aoi stretched out her slim arm and
pointed to the path leading to the front
of the house. The gesture could have
but one meaning. Young Saunders
flushed angrily.

"This is a deuce of a way to take a
fellow's attentions," he said, half to himself. "Why, I declare, I meant no
harm."

Aoi smiled incredulously.

"I am old," she said, slowly; and at
her flushed, almost youthful, face the
young man smiled involuntarily. But
she repeated her words: "I am old with
experience, Mister—sir—and because I
was the wife of an Englishman, I know
from him the evil meant by such attention as yours to a maiden of Japan."

"But she is not Japanese," he burst
out; "I never for a moment thought of
her as such."

His words staggered Aoi. In her zeal

167

to protect the girl from the overtures of this foreigner she had forgotten the facts of the girl's birth. She became agitated. Her hands fell helplessly to her knees as she bent brokenly forward. With her head bowed, she spoke in a plaintive voice:

"The humble one craves the pardon of the illustrious sir. But will he not condescend to depart?"

Somewhat irritated and provoked, rather sulkily he turned towards the path and slowly, unwillingly, left the garden.

XVIII

A MONTH and a half had gone by since the American attorney had cabled to his client in Europe of the success of his mission. Richard Lorrimer's immediate response had been that he was leaving at once for Japan. Any day now he might arrive in Sendai.

In the meanwhile, Aoi sought to comfort and strengthen the despairing Hyacinth. She contrived to break up their retirement, and sought to divert her mind by taking her out each day. The girl had acquired a peculiar loathing and horror for the "white people," of whom the little town of Sendai had now quite a plague.

The women went about in hideous garments, with what appeared to be heavy flower-baskets upon their heads.

169

The men gazed at her and made insinuating efforts to speak to her. Hyacinth was sure all these foreigners carried knives, because they were constantly chipping off pieces of the tombs and the temples. They were sacrilegious beasts, she thought, who had not reverence even for the dead. Everywhere in the city she found them. Sometimes they were even on the heights of Matsushima, where they laughed and talked in loud voices to one another under the very shadows of the holy temples. She hated them all, she told herself. Most of all she loathed this man who was said to be her father, who had broken her mother's heart and married a woman her mother despised, and who now sought to drag her by force from those she loved.

Yet the visiting foreigners in Sendai possessed a more friendly spirit towards her than she knew. Knowing her history, they were prompted by pity and curiosity to seek an acquaintance, which was always met by the darkest and

haughtiest of frowns and disdainful
glances. When they addressed her, she
stared stonily before her. Once, when
a too-curious woman persisted in annoy-
ing her with numerous questions, Hyacinth had raised her voice suddenly and
shrieked to a score of little urchins playing in the street. In an instant they
had rushed into the road, whence they
threw sticks and mud at the indignant
foreigner. Whereat Hyacinth had burst
into a wild peal of shrill, defiant laughter.
Then she had rushed headlong into the
house, where she flung herself on the
floor, giving vent to a tempest of tears.

In these days she could not bear Aoi
out of her sight, and even old Mumè received an unusual share of affection. The
thought of leaving them caused her deep
sorrow. The passage of the days added
not one whit to her resignation. If she
must go, she would go battling at every
step. But, before the time should come,
maybe the gods would intervene, and she
might die.

171

Strangely enough, in these days she forgot, or refused to remember, all she had learned at the mission-house. Instead, she would climb wearily the long way to one of the temples on the hill, where she sought the old priest who kept the fire of the gods perpetually burning, and bitterly she poured out at his feet all the anguish of her heart.

She was a Japanese girl, she asserted— Japanese in thought, in feeling, in heart, in soul. How could she leave her beloved home and people to go away with these cold, white ones, whom she could never, never learn to know or understand.

And the priest promised to give her counsel and help when the time should come. From day to day he would admonish:

"A little longer—wait! The gods will find a way."

But the days passed with more than natural speed of time. Then came a telegram to Sendai. The lawyer, Mr.

Knowles, brought it to Aoi's house. It was from Mr. Lorrimer. He had arrived in Tokyo. He would start at once for Sendai.

Then desperation seized upon Hyacinth. Unmindful of the pleadings of Aoi, she besought the Yamashiro family for help.

Now, the Yamashiro family had always been ashamed of the fact that Hyacinth was half English. They had more than once declared that if she had been wholly so a union with their son would have been an impossible thing. Consequently, Madame Yamashiro received the young girl frigidly. She considered it both hoydenish and rude for a girl to pay a visit to her betrothed's parents alone. But the moment Hyacinth began to speak, Madame Yamashiro became so frightened that she trembled.

The girl, in a breath, told her of the discovery of her true parentage. She implored Madame Yamashiro to hasten her marriage with Yoshida, so that she might not be forced to leave Japan. For could this foreign father then tear her from her husband? No, all the laws of Japan would prevent him.

So rapid was her utterance that one word tripped against another.

In her agitation, Madame Yamashiro thought the girl insane. She clapped her hands so loudly that half a dozen maidens came to answer at once.

"The master!" she cried; and never had the Yamashiro servants seen their mistress so perturbed.

Not a word did she speak to Hyacinth after that until her husband and son entered the room; then faithfully she repeated the words of the girl.

Like a little stupid animal the boy's round face became vacant. He stared at the girl out of a pair of small, amazed eyes. She tapped her foot impatiently upon the floor, and then turned to the father, her two little hands outstretched.

"Oh, good Yamashiro, will you not

hasten this marriage? I am ready, willing, to wed at once — to-day — this minute."

"If it be true," said Yamashiro, heavily, "that you are an Engleesh, it is quite impossible. My son could not marry with such."

"But we are betrothed," she cried, piteously. "Yamashiro Yoshida is my affianced. Oh, you will not cast me off!"

She turned pitifully from one to the other. They were all quite silent. Then she spoke to Yoshida. Her voice was clear and hard.

"You—Yoshida, you would not cast me off? You swore you adored me. It is not my fault I am Engleesh. I am Japanese here."

She placed her hands over her heart.

"If you will marry me," she said, "I will be Japanese altogether."

"My son," said Yamashiro the elder, "will obey his father's august will in all things."

175

The girl spoke slowly, scornfully.

"I make a fool of myself to come to you with such a request. I would not marry you, Yoshida—no, not though the white people killed me."

Drawing the doors sharply behind her, Hyacinth left the house unattended to the gate.

"Ah, what an escape we have had!" burst from Madame Yamashiro.

Her husband scowled.

Yoshida slowly moved to the shoji and stared out dimly at the little figure hurrying down the path.

XIX

"YAMASHIRO YOSHIDA will not marry
me. He has cast me off," Hyacinth
told Aoi.

"And to-night," said Aoi, helplessly,
"the father will arrive."

The girl pressed her hands tightly together. Aoi laid a timid, comforting
hand upon her shoulder.

"Little one," she said, in a pleading
voice, "pray thee to take cheer. It is
your duty to go to your father. You
have not forgotten all I have taught
you. Filial submission to the parent is
the most important of all."

"And have I not always shown such
respect and devotion to you, dear
mother?"

"To me? Ah, yes, little one, and I

would that I were, indeed, your own mother."

"You are, you are," cried the girl, crushing down the sob that rose in her throat, and then dashing her hand against her eyes. "Ah," she cried, "this is not time to weep. We must think—must think of some way. Yamashiro has failed us. Ah! Who could have expected else? They were always despicable."

"Try and follow my counsel," said Aoi; "accept the inevitable. The father is coming; he is your rightful guardian. Bow to his will and give him what affection you can."

"I can give him not one grain of affection," said the girl, bitterly. "Did he not cast off my mother for that other woman? Ah, I have heard all the story. What I could not understand that first day I have learned since, and you also. Did you not tell me that my mother died shuddering at his memory?"

Aoi sighed helplessly. The girl threw

178

herself down on the floor, and, resting her chin upon her hand, stared out before her at the street without. There had been a little rain, and the bamboo trees across the street were shining with the drops which had not yet dried upon them.

Looking down the street, she could see the dim outline of the country beyond, the cloud-shaped mountains, the sheen of the water beneath. She turned back to Aoi, who had silently seated herself beside her.

"Mother," she said, "I am going away alone."

"Alone! Ah, you make my heart stand still with fear."

"Listen. All Matsushima is known to me, and the priests at the temple are kind and love me. If I need food they will give it to me. Do they not feed even the birds which alight upon their temples?"

"Oh, child, I cannot think what it is you contemplate."

"I will not leave our Japan," she cried, passionately. "It is the only home I have known."

"But what can you do?"

"I will hide," said the girl.

"Ah, alas, you could not, for these foreigners are everywhere here. They would find you."

"Yet there are places among the tombs of Date of which they know naught. Koma and I alone knew of them, and the good priest of the temple Zuiganjii. There is one place—but I will not tell even you."

Aoi wrung her hands.

"Oh, daughter, they will seek everywhere for you till they find you. You do not know the stubborn nature of these people."

"Ah, but I do, my mother, for that nature is in me, too. If they seek stubbornly, I, too, can hide as well."

Arising, she stood a moment, looking down thoughtfully upon Aoi.

"To-night," she said, "they will come.

180

There is little time to lose. When they ask for me, you will say, 'She feared to gaze upon the augustness of her parent, and so fled.' When they ask you, 'Where fled?' you will say, 'Only the gods know whither.'"

XX

THE great red sun had finished its day of travel and had dropped deep into the waters far off in the gilded western sky. How very still were the approaching shadows, how phantom-like they seemed to creep, spreading, though they scarcely stirred. The glow of the sun was still upon the land, reflecting the light on the dew-damped trees and the upturned faces of the nameless flowers, which seemed to raise their heads, hungry, as though loath to part with the light.

Not a sound was heard on Matsushima. The birds were voiceless, the waters moved with a soundless motion, licking rather than beating against the rocks, stirring lazily, as if in slumber.

Upon the silence there tenderly stole

the gentle, mellow pealing of a temple bell. Its even-song was soft and sweetly muffled, so that one would have thought it came from afar off.

Hyacinth, heartsick and footsore, was weary when she reached the bay. With a little cry she caught her breath, as for the first time she looked about her, awakened from her apathy by the sudden tone of the bell.

The light of day was disappearing. Already the hills up which she must climb looked dark and in ghostly contrast to the still light and shining bay. Yet the girl lingered on the shore, her hand shading her eyes, watching yearningly the sunset. The beauty of the passing day hurt her. She was in a condition to feel acutely. The temple bell had ceased its song. With the departure of the sun, the silence seemed more oppressive.

Shuddering now, she looked up fearfully at the hills. Not since she was a very little child had she visited these particular hills at night, and even then she had not been alone.

Yet in those days she could have found her way blindfolded among the rocks, stupendously projecting and facing the silent bay. She had assured Aoi that she knew every inch of the land hereabouts. Yet now, as she turned from the shore of the bay and began to climb upward, she stumbled uncertainly. Her hands, outstretched before her, revealed the fact that she was blindly feeling her way, and wandering along paths she did not know.

"It will be all right soon," she kept repeating to herself. "I am not lost; only a little dazed, and I am tired— tired. Wait, I will find the great rock soon, and then all will be well with me."

She wandered about hither and thither in the darkness. Gigantic rocks were about her on all sides, now shutting out the light of the bay. Behind her the hills loomed up into enormous mountains, steep and impenetrable.

The darkness about her, accentuated by the shadows of the rocks, awed and terrified her. She raised her face appealingly to the sky. Only one star shone out in its firmanent, bright, soft, and luminous.

"It is becoming lighter," she said. "Ah, will the moon never arise?"

And, as she spoke, the lazy moon crept upward beyond the black mountains, a train of stars following in her wake. Her light was bright, and reflected in a silver gleam upon the upturned face of Hyacinth.

Light was all about her. The black shadows had evaporated like the mist, and clean cut about her the familiar cliffs and rocks outjutted, and the white tombs of the great feudal lords of Sendai shone out like strange, unearthly mirrors. She stood in their midst, close by the deserted Zuiganjii. And the rock against which she leaned grew suddenly white and dazzling. Gazing with awed, wondering eyes upon

185

it, she thought that some kindly goddess had guided her wandering footsteps in the dark to the very refuge she sought.

Yet she did not enter the cavern beneath, though she was weary. She was watching, with reverential emotion, one of the phenomena of nature. As she looked upward she knew that this sight would bring that evening to Matsushima's shore hundreds of banqueters, for the Japanese never fail to celebrate the Milky Way. They call it the Heavenly River, in which goddesses wash their robes in the month of August.

Mechanically, and almost unconsciously, she climbed to the surface of the rock. From her height she now looked down upon the bay. Across the waters on the other shore the temples were illuminated. The white sails of some fishing-boats were floating like white birds gently swimming.

For a time she stood quietly on the great rock. The silence and stillness of the night possessed her, and she became drowsy. She stooped and touched the surface of the rock, and found that it was covered with some soft moss.

"It is so dark inside," she said, plaintively, "and I am so weary. The gods will give me sleep without."

In a little while her tired little body had relaxed its tension. She lay there on the rock, upon her back, her arms stretched far out on either side, like the wings of a bird, her face upturned to the white-flecked sky.

Thus, among the tombs of the ancient lords of Sendai, upon the very rock where the Date lords met to raise their voices in allegiance to the religion of her ancestors, this little Caucasian maiden slept alone.

XI

MADAME AOI was fluttering from room to room, her face anxious, her whole being disturbed and agitated. Although she knew that the expected guests might arrive at any minute, she could not remain still a moment.

In and out of Hyacinth's chamber she wandered, distracted, and with the yearning pain of a mother wringing her heart. The little room, with its dainty, pretty mattings, its exquisite panellings, seemed to reflect the personality of the loved one who had left her to bitter loneliness. Even the sunlight seemed less golden now that she was gone, and the dressing - table, with its mirror, propped up by a lacquer stick behind it, had a forlorn appearance.

Everything about the chamber, about

the whole house, bore a deserted aspect.
Aoi was not one given to the indulgence
of tears, but her quiet pain was all the
more acute. Her appealing face was
drawn and devoid of all color. The
anguish of her heart was manifest in her
eyes and in her quivering lips.

Once she opened the panelling and
looked for a moment within at the
clothes of the dead mother. She drew
back the panel almost sharply. The
sight of those dumb, silent articles
struck her with a nameless horror.
Woman-like, she recalled the face of the
one to whom they had belonged. Then
she began to conjure up fancies of
what this mother would have desired
her to do with her child. And the face
which returned to her memory seemed,
somehow, to reproach her with its sad
and melancholy eyes.

For the first time since she had adopted Hyacinth, poor, childish Aoi began
to doubt whether she had done right.
Did not the little one, after all, belong to

these people? Was it not, therefore, wrong to have kept her in ignorance of them, and permitted her to grow to maidenhood after the fashion of a Japanese girl? This emotional arraignment caused Aoi anguish.

Time now hung heavily upon her; the minutes seemed to creep. She stared out at the graying sky, and wondered where the little one was now. At that moment Hyacinth had halted in her pilgrimage on the shore of the bay to gaze upon the same sunset, wistfully, yearningly.

The sight of the fading day aroused a fear in the breast of the watching Aoi. She sprang to her feet, smoothed her gown with hasty, trembling hands, and moved towards the street door.

She would go to the mission-house people and tell her story. They might assist her, advise her what course to pursue. They had always taken deep interest in the little one. Perhaps they, too, loved her. Oh, if anything should happen to her, out there in the darkness of the hills!

Aoi had hardly reached the foot of the little spiral stairs when there were sharp rappings upon the door. With her hand pressed tight to her fluttering heart, she hastened forward. Without waiting for the slow Mumè to answer the summons, she pushed the door aside.

Then she stood still, dumbly, on the threshold. The next instant Komazawa had seized her in his arms and was covering her face with kisses. Against her son's breast she began to sob in a helpless, hopeless fashion, piteous to see.

He, with his arm close about her, comforted softly, and then turning to the strangers who were with him, he said, quietly:

"You see my unexpected arrival has upset my mother. You must excuse the welcome. But, come, let us enter."

The man and woman, exchanging

191

glances, followed the young man and his
mother into the guest-room.

The woman was tall and had once
been pretty. She was faded now, and
her blond hair was dull and streaked,
showing the effects of having once been
bleached. The man was well preserved,
but bore the evidence of rich living in
the somewhat reddened and bloated appearance of eyes and cheeks. His hair
was gray and he wore a short imperial.
Just now his expression was one of
extreme uneasiness. His lips twitched
nervously, and his brow was drawn.
He had long, slender, white hands, the
fingers nicotine stained. He had a
straight, military figure, and was dressed in a rather *outré* manner.

Aoi regarded him with undisguised
fearfulness. She had no notion who
these strangers could be, yet there was
something in the man's restless attitude
that aroused her apprehensions. She
turned anxiously to her son. He was
grave and pale.

"Mother," he said, "this is Mr. and Mrs. Lorrimer. You have been expecting them, I believe."

Aoi was so moved that she could only bow feebly to her visitors.

Her son's voice was low and, to her agitated fancy, strained.

"Mother," he said, "why was I not informed of the claims made by—Mr. Lorrimer?"

"Oh, son, I feared to tell you," she replied, tremulously; "the little one besought me not to do so."

"It was only by accident," he said, "that I learned the facts. We happened to cross on the same steamer, and, somehow, Mr. Lorrimer confided in me."

Aoi clung to her son's hand, but she did not speak. Her face was raised to his as though she listened eagerly to every word he uttered.

"I came back to Japan," he said, "for another purpose—to prevent, if I could, Hyacinth's marriage. It was entirely without my approval. I consider her

193

little more than a child. However, I shortly discovered that I had no right to dictate to her even in this matter. Her father—'' He indicated, slightly, Mr. Lorrimer, who seized the opportunity to step forward.

He spoke jerkily and somewhat impatiently.

''It seems to me that we are wasting time. You will, I am sure, perceive my intense anxiety to see my—er—daughter.''

''I beg your pardon for detaining you. It was very stupid of me.'' Komazawa turned back to Aoi.

''Where is she, mother?'' he asked, simply.

Silently Aoi shook her drooped head. She could not speak.

''Where is she?'' repeated Koma, now with a slight thrill of apprehension in his voice.

Still that silent, drooping little figure, with its bowed head and lips that refused to speak.

194

The shadows deepened in the room, and without the skies were darkening.

Aoi raised her head, shivered, and looked about her dazedly. Then suddenly she clapped her hands mechanically.

She was sending for the girl, thought the other three, as they waited in tense silence for a response to her summons. But when Mumè thrust in her fat, reddened face, Aoi only mechanically said :

"Lights, honorable maid."

Koma placed his hand heavily on her shoulder.

"Mother," he said, "you do not make me answer.   Where is Hyacinth?"

"Gone," said Aoi, faintly.

"Gone!   What do you mean?"

"Ah, excellencies," she cried, turning to the visitors and speaking in broken English, "the liddle one's heart broke at thought of leaving her home.   She is still but a child, and she had a child's fear of meeting—of meeting strangers,

195

and so—and so—she went, excellencies,
she—"

"Ran away," said the woman. "Well,
what do you think of that?" She turned her lip ever so slightly, pushing the
point of her parasol into Aoi's immac-
ulate matting. "Runs in the family,
apparently," she said.

Ignoring her utterly, Mr. Lorrimer addressed Aoi in a hoarse voice:

"When did she go, and where? You
must know."

"She went, illustrious excellency, only
a little while ago."

"Where? You know?"

"Nay, I do not know, save that she
has gone to the hills. But, oh, excellency, there are so many hills, so large,
so dense! Can we find the one ant by
searching in its hill? Who can find the
little one among the monstrous hills?"

"I can," said Komazawa, stepping
forward suddenly.

Aoi rushed to him frantically.

"Oh, son," she cried, in Japanese, "do

196

not assist these strangers. Do not track the little one to give her to them. You will not take part with them against us?"

"Mother," he answered, in Japanese, "you do wrong in speaking thus. You misjudge me. It is not to assist these people I would search for her. No, though they had a thousand claims on her. But I must go to save her from herself. The cliffs on the hills are perilous, and the night would frighten the little one. It is for that reason I would seek her."

He caught up his hat and made to leave the room, but again his mother stayed him.

"Oh, son, in such a garb you would frighten the little one."

He paused in thought a moment, then turned in the opposite direction.

"It is true. My room—it is as ever?"

"As ever, son. Always awaiting thy return."

He vanished through the folding-doors. They heard him speeding rapidly up the stairs.

"Where has he gone?" asked Mrs. Lorrimer, sharply.

"To arrange his dress," the Japanese woman answered, without raising her head.

"Oh, such folly!" she cried, angrily. "There is no time to be lost. He should start at once. What shall we do?"

This last question she shot at her husband, who was staring miserably before him.

"I don't know, I'm sure," he said, dejectedly. "I declare, I'm quite—quite done up."

"Well, I know what to do," she said. "We must look up those mission-house people and have a search-party sent out at once. We can get no satisfaction from these people. Come."

XXII

It was nearly midnight when Komazawa passed along the shore of Matsushima and began to climb towards the tombs. He knew every inch of the land. Unlike poor, wandering Hyacinth, he passed steadily ahead without the slightest hesitation. He had reached the small cliff path which led to the great Date-rock cavern. Now he was before the rock itself.

Without pausing an instant, holding the lighted lantern he carried above his head, he entered the cavern beneath the rock. Every inch of the ground within he examined, feeling about with his hands in the darkened corners where his lantern could not penetrate. Over and over the same ground he went, fear urging him forward. When the certain-

ty that she was not within the cavern
forced itself upon him his shaking frame
testified to his agitation.

He had been so certain that the girl
would come here. This was the great
secret cave he himself had shown to her,
where they had spent their childhood
together in defiance of the mild re-
monstrance of the temple priests.

Very slowly now Koma crawled from
out the cavern. The lantern he set
upon the ground at the mouth of the
cave. Then he stood still, uncertain
what to do, a great despair coming upon
him.

Only a few paces away, he knew, were
other tombs and caverns, but these were
built in the slanting cliffs, down which
no maiden could have gone in safety.
Of them he would not think. He dared
not look at them, lest he become dizzy
with horror. And so Komazawa raised
his face upward to the sky, just as
Hyacinth had done.

Then he saw, far up above his head,

something dark and still outstretched
upon the surface of the rock. He caught
his breath, then covered his mouth with
his hands lest a cry escape him. Slowly
and carefully he climbed up to the
surface of the rock. A moment, on its
edge, he paused irresolute, then crept
on his knees towards the sleeping girl.

For a long time he knelt in a rapt
silence beside her, his eyes fixed, entranced, upon her face.

She was slumbering as calmly as
a child, and her upturned face, with
the moon-rays upon it, was wondrous-
ly, ethereally beautiful. Awed, reverential, Koma gazed upon the picture, then
soundlessly he crept back to the edge
of the rock and clambered down. Once
more he stood on the ground below.
His face had a strange, strained expression, and in his eyes gleamed a new
light.

"I cannot awaken her," he said to
himself, "and oh, ye gods! how beautiful
she has grown!"

For a time he stood there without moving, plunged in reverie. Then his eyes, wandering mechanically towards the bay, fell on a series of lights on the shore below. They were one behind the other, and swung back and forth. In an instant he recognized them. The next moment he had thrust his own light into the cavern.

"They will not come this way," he assured himself. "This ancient path is little known save to the priests. Yet —if they should!"

He clinched his hands tensely at his side and stood off a few paces, looking up at the top of the rock.

"It is very high up, and—they might not see. As I did—they might pass by."

He leaned far over, straining his eyes to pierce through the shadows beneath. The lights below flashed a moment from out some foliage, disappeared behind some rocks, reappeared again, and then plunged into a forest path which led,

Koma knew, far from his present position.

He heaved a great sigh of relief.

"Ah, it is well—well," he said; "yet, nevertheless, I must watch — I must guard her."

XXIII

WITH stealing step morning crept up on Matsushima. The sky had scarcely paled to a slumberous gray ere the soft, yellow streaks of the sun shot upward in the east, tinting all the land with its glow. The morning star was poised on high, as though lingering to watch the sun's awakening. Then, softly, it twinkled out into the vapor.

Hyacinth stirred on her strange couch, her eyelashes quivered sleepily against her cheeks. One little hand opened a moment, then clutched the dew-wet moss. The touch of the unfamiliar grass against her hand startled her, and the girl opened her eyes. They looked upward at the softly bluing sky. A breeze of morning swept across her brow, moving a little truant curl. She

204

sat up and stared about her wonder-
ingly. Then remembrance coming to
her, she sat still, silently watching the
sunrise. For some moments she remained in this absorbed silence. Then
mechanically she raised her hands to her
head and sought to smooth the soft hair
that the breeze had ruffled.

"How still it is!" she said. Then, a
moment after, "Heu! the rock is so hard,
and it is chilly." She shivered.

Then moving along the rock, she came
to the edge and began to clamber down.
There were clefts in the rock which
Koma had cut as a boy, and she had no
difficulty in descending. She dropped
to the ground as lightly as a bird. Turning about, a sudden little cry escaped her
lips.

She stood as if rooted to the ground,
regarding with dilated eyes the figure
before her. He did not speak. His
eyes were upon her face, and he was
watching her startled expression with
an eager glance. Then she took a step

towards him, holding out both her hands.

"Komazawa!" she cried. "It is you!"

He did not touch her outstretched hands, and she shrank back as if struck.

"You, too!" she said, and her hand sought her head bewilderedly.

"I, too?" he repeated, stupidly.

"Yes," she cried. "I understand why you are here, why you do not speak to me and embrace me as of old. Ah, it is all very plain."

"What is very plain?" he asked, still keeping his distance from her.

"Why you are here. They have sent you to find me, to give me over to those strangers. It is cruel, cruel!" she cried, covering her face with her hands.

"It is not true!" he cried, going to her and taking her hands from her face and holding them closely in his own.

She did not seek to release them, but permitted them to remain passively in his, as she looked up into his face through her tears.

"It is not true," he repeated, softly.

"Yet you were not glad to see me," she said, tremulously.

"Ah, but I was," he replied, in that same soft, subtle voice which, somehow, vaguely thrilled her.

"You did not speak to me."

"Your face—your sudden appearance —startled me; I could not speak for a moment," he said.

"Yet even now," she said, catching her breath, "you do not embrace me."

He dropped her hands slowly and drew back a pace.

"It would not be right—now," he said, huskily.

"I do not understand," she said. "Have we not always embraced each other?"

"We were children before," he said, "but now—embraces are for—for lovers only."

She looked at him a long moment in wondering silence, a slow, pink glow spreading gradually over her face. Then she repeated, slowly, almost falteringly:

"For—for lovers!"

He turned his eyes away from her face. She put a timid hand upon his arm.

"Yet," she said, "Yamashiro Yoshida was my lover, and—and we did not embrace."

"Ah, no, thank the Heavens!" he cried, impetuously, again possessing himself of her hands. "You were safe from such things here, little one. Yet you have much to learn — much, and I—" His eyes became purple and his chin squared in strong resolution. "I'm going to teach you," he said.

"Teach me?" she faltered. "What will you teach me?"

"The meaning of love," he said, the words escaping him as if he could not control them.

"You will be my lover?" she said, timid wonder in her eyes.

He could not speak for some moments. Then—

208

"Ah, what have I been saying? Little one, you do not know, you cannot dream of the extent of your own innocence. I would be less than man if your words did not pierce my heart and thrill my whole being. Yet I am not altogether selfish — no — though I have spent years of my life among those who were so. I will not take advantage of the little one. She shall have every opportunity her birth, her beauty, demands. You will go with your father, Hyacinth. Nay, do not interrupt me. It will be for your good. You must see this other world, to which you rightfully belong. Then when you have come to years of womanhood you can decide for yourself."

"I am already a woman," she said, tremulously.

"Only a child—a little girl," he said, softly; "a poor little one who has been imprisoned so long she has come to believe her own cage is gilded, and will not take her freedom when the doors are opened."

Earnestly she looked into his face.

"And if I go to the West country, you, too, will go with me, will you not, Koma?"

He shook his head, smiling sadly.

"No. I would not have the right."

"I will not go, then," she said, simply. "If they should force me I can be as brave as others. I would take my life."

"No, you would not do so, for then you would break our hearts."

"Yet you have no pity for mine," she said, near to tears now.

"Poor little heart!" he whispered, tenderly.

After a moment she inquired, quietly:

"And did you come with my august parent, then?"

"On the same steamer—yes. It was an accidental meeting."

"Ah, then you did not come back for the purpose of helping them?"

"No, I had another purpose. I came to break your betrothal with Yamashiro Yoshida."

"Well, they have saved you that trouble," she said, sighing.

He regarded her keenly.

"Why do you sigh? You have regrets?"

"Yes," she admitted, "for if they had not cast me off I could have remained in Japan. Now—" Her voice faltered and she turned her head away.

"Now?" he repeated.

"Ah, yes," she said, "I begin to see there is nothing else to be done. I am resigned."

"You are resigned," he repeated, disappointment showing in his transparent face.

"Yes," she said, with a fleeting upward glance at his face.

She suddenly laughed quite merrily.

"Come," she said, "let us go home. I must humbly submit myself to the august will of my honorable parent."

Koma said never a word. Manlike, he was regretting his late words of advised self-sacrifice.

XXIV

IT was a slow pilgrimage homeward that these two young people made, for they stopped at every familiar place on the hills and by the bay that they had known as children. And, like children, they dipped their faces in the shining water of the little brook that wound its way around the hills and fell in a tiny waterfall below into the bay.

They slipped into a darkened temple, touching with reverent, loving fingers the deserted images within. At the little village on the shore, where they had lived together as children, they halted and lunched at a tiny tavern whose garden was the shore of the bay. And when they had struck the road that led to Sendai they turned their steps backward and wandered along the white beach of Matsushima.

The girl, whose heart had been so heavy for days with the thought of leaving her home, now with the light-heartedness of a child seemed to have forgotten all her troubles and to revel in the joy of living.

But a gentle melancholy was upon Komazawa. It was with something of reproach that he answered the merry chatter of his companion.

"Yonder," she said, pointing across the bay, while her long sleeve, falling back, disclosed her soft, dimpled arm, "is the naked island Hadakajima. See, it is not changed at all, Koma. Do you remember those times when you would carry me on your shoulder and step from rock to rock in the bay until you had reached Hadaka-jima?"

"Yes," he said, watching her eyes.

She looked up at him sideways, then drooped her lashes downward.

"You would not do the same to-day?" she said.

"You are not the same—child," he replied.

"Ah, no," she sighed. "I am changed, alas!"

"Why 'alas'?"

"The change does not please you," she said.

"Ah, but it does."

"Yet you were kinder to me then."

He did not reply. She raised her face.

"Is it not so?"

"Perhaps," he replied.

"Then you must have loved me more then," she said.

"No, that is not true."

"No? Do you still love me, then?"

"I cannot answer you," he said. "If I were to tell you my heart you would not believe me, because you would not understand."

"Ah, but I would, indeed," she said, softly.

214

"You are innocent," he said, regarding her thoughtfully, "but you are a coquette by nature."

"What is that?"

"One who makes a jest of love."

"And what is love?"

"Your heart will tell you some day."

"Yet I would have your heart tell me now."

"Love is a rosy pain of the heart."

"Then I do not feel it," she said, stretching out her little, pink fingers over her heart, "for mine thrills and beats with joyous palpitations. Yet " — she looked up at him seriously—"perhaps that, too, is another of the moods of this love."

"Perhaps," he said. "Love is capricious."

Hyacinth sighed and looked out wistfully across the bay.

"It is a strange word," she said, vaguely.

"Yes, strange," he said. "I have lived years in England, but I had to return to Nippon to learn its meaning."

"Yet you have been back but a day," she said, tremulously.

"And love is born in a moment," he whispered, and took her hand softly in his own.

She withdrew it quickly, and turned from him in a sudden panic of incomprehensible fear, the morning had wrought such a change in her.

"We must be going home," she said. "Nay, we must hurry."

And after that they walked homeward swiftly in silence, each afraid to speak to the other.

XXV

As Hyacinth passed up the little garden-path she saw a familiar face at the open shoji of the guest-room.

"It is Yamashiro Yoshida," she said to Koma.

"What does he want?" her companion demanded, with such unexpected harshness that the girl broke into a silvery peal of laughter.

"The gods alone know. We shall see. Ah, but he is welcome!"

Aoi met them at the door. Her poor, little, anxious face hurt the girl more than if she had heaped her with reproaches. With an unwonted tenderness she threw her arms about the mother's neck and pressed her face against hers, whispering over and over again.

"How I love you! It is so good to see you again."

"Yoshida is within," said Aoi, when the girl had released her. "He comes alone."

"What!" she cried, in mock surprise. "The brave Yoshida ventures out alone? Well, and what does he want?"

"Nay, he would not tell me. He will speak only to you, little one."

"Very well. Let him speak," and she pushed the doors gayly aside and entered the oxashishi. She was not aware that Koma had entered also until, following the glance of Yoshida, she perceived Koma behind her. Then her voice rippled merrily, and she spoke affectionately to Yamashiro Yoshida.

"Why, Yamashiro Yoshida, what brings you here? I had not dreamed of the blessings the gods had in store for me. I am so affected by the light of your presence that I am rendered speechless," which last was quite un-

218

true, as both the young men could have attested.

Yoshida bowed himself to the ground; and now, oblivious of the presence of the intruder, Koma, replied:

"Ah, beauteous one, I am come to bring you a most insignificant present, and to beseech you to pardon the rudeness of my family and to permit our betrothal to continue."

The girl took the gift slowly and held it on the palm of her hand. It was a very exquisitely lacquered box, and she knew without opening it that it contained some very valuable complexion powder. Her lover, however, could not have told from her face the effect of his words and gift upon her.

Her eyes were inscrutable, her lips pressed closely together. She seemed to be examining the box with critical eyes, as though she were weighing its value.

Without a word of response, she suddenly crossed to the tokonona and drew out from underneath it a fairly large box. Its contents she removed slowly, setting the articles in a semicircle on the floor about her. Soon she was quite encircled by the contents. Then, with one little, pointing finger, she spoke:

"This obi, Yamashiro Yoshida, was your first gift. It was given on the day of our betrothal. I have never worn it. It was too rich for one so small as I."

She looked full into the face of Yoshida, and then with a fleeting glance she saw the face of Koma. She smiled ever so sweetly.

"These pins, Yoshida, are costly, but murderous appearing. Once they pricked my head."

She stuck them into the sash of the obi.

"These bracelets," she said, "are just exactly like the ones you gave to the geisha Morning Glory."

She laid them beside the pins.

"This kimono, honorable Yoshida, is

220

so heavy its weight would break the back of one so humble as I."

"Lady," said Yamashiro Yoshida, haughtily, "you make a jest of my gifts. I assure you I do not appreciate it. Why do you thus enumerate them? Is it not ungracious?"

Sweetly the girl swept all of the gifts into a heap together, then, rising with them in her arms, she crossed to Yoshida.

"Yamashiro Yoshida," she said, "I never loved you, yet I betrothed myself to you because of the magnificence of your gifts. I was an ignorant child. Then you and your august parents cast me off because of my honorable origin, which you despised. Now you come to attempt to buy me with another gift. But I am no longer a silly child, and I give you back not only that new gift, but—all—all—all—all. Take them —take them quickly."

She thrust them into his arms. Angrily he attempted to refuse them. They fell crashing to the floor. A man's rich voice suddenly broke out into laughter.

"It is an insult!" cried Yamashiro Yoshida, furiously, trampling upon his gifts, half by accident, half blindly. He glared at the sweetly smiling face of the girl—glared at the laughing Komazawa; then he clapped his hands violently.

"My shoes!" he fairly shouted at Mumè, as she answered his summons.

He kicked his feet into his shoes, stamped on the floor furiously, then turned on his heel and left the house in a fine rage.

XXVI

As the irate Yoshida vanished through the doors, Hyacinth clapped her hands with a childish gesture of delight. She looked at Koma, now regarding her gravely, then, with a dimpling smile, she sat down on the mats among the despised gifts. These she tossed about gayly.

"He has gone away," she said, "mad as three devils of Osaka, but what matter? He has left the gifts! Such a silly lover, such a foolish one!"

She began to collect the gifts, folding the obi and the rich kimono.

"You are not going to keep them?" said Koma, standing over her and looking down at her gravely.

"Not going to keep them? Why, the lover refused to accept their return."

"Yes, but you don't want them."

"But I do," she protested, patting the folded obi lovingly.

"Why, you told him you did not."

"Oh," she said, airily. "That's just foolish pride. I was just talking — through my head."

She laughed mischievously.

"That's liddle slang I learned at mission-house," she said.

"I want you to send those presents back to this Yamashiro."

"Send all those lovely presents back?"

She shook her head.

"Could not do it," she said. "Too great sacrifice."

"I will buy you all the things you want."

She stared up at him amazedly.

"You?"

"Yes," he replied, flushing, "I—why not?"

"Well, but "—she regarded him doubtfully—"you are not rich like Yamashiro Yoshida."

224

"How do you know?" he asked, quietly.

She regarded him dubiously.

"When I get those presents from you," she said, "then I will return these. That right?"

He pulled the box over to the centre of the floor, and thrust the gifts into it, snapping the lid down tightly. Then, going to the door, he called for Mumè to take the box at once to the Yamashiros.

Having disposed of this question, he turned his attention again to Hyacinth. She was sitting in the centre of the room, her chin on her hand, pensively regarding him.

"How," she said, "are you going to make me those gifts if I am to go away to that West country, and you will not go with me?"

"You are going to stay here," he said; and she knew from the expression in his eyes and the tone of his voice that he meant what he said.

"But what of my august parent?"

225

"Will you follow my advice exactly?"
She nodded in assent.

"When he comes you are to make a request of him."

"Yes?"

"Ask him—beg him even—to permit you to remain one month in Sendai with us. Then tell him that after that you will go wherever your rightful guardian shall direct."

"He will not consent," she said, depression seizing upon her—"these august barbarians are hard as rock. They never move—no, never."

"Who told you that?"

"Nobody," she said, "but I observe."

"Where did you observe it?" he persisted.

She looked at him sideways a moment without replying. Then she dimpled and smiled.

"In the mission-house people and in —you, Koma," she said.

"Promise me that you will make the request?"

"Very well, I will make that foolish promise. But "—she thrust out a little red underlip in a bewitching pout— "one month will soon come to an end, and after that?"

"After that you will leave the rest to me," he said.

XXVII

In the guest-room of Madame Aoi's house, the Lorrimers had waited fully a half-hour. Their patience was wellnigh exhausted. Lorrimer's nervousness and anxiety threatened to result in utter collapse. The events of the last few months, through which this dissipated man of the world had suddenly found himself to be the father of a child he had never seen, and by the woman his conscience had never ceased to tell him he had wronged, were having their effect upon him.

He was a weak-natured man, easily ruled through his affections; but he was not bad-hearted. Many years ago the woman who was now his wife had prevailed upon him to divorce another wife that he might marry her. Richard

Lorrimer's affection for his second wife had evaporated during the honeymoon, and was flameless and dead in twelve months. Since then his life with her had been dull, aimless, purposeless, broken in its monotony only at intervals by the woman's spasmodic efforts to fan the flame into life.

Now a strange and novel emotion was stirring the soul—if soul it could be called in such a nature — of Richard Lorrimer. He had a feverish, almost childish, longing to see, to possess, this child—his own. He was too sluggish and indolent by nature to have an imagination which would have pictured her in his mind. He had a hazy idea that she would be like any other American child, that she would, of course, be shy of him at first, but that the natural feeling of a child for its father would assert its power. He felt certain that she would prove a source of pleasure and comfort to him.

Nervously he paced the floor, with

irregular, broken strides, stopping now and then to look about him, or to answer the impatient remarks that escaped his wife's lips.

"This is beautiful," she said. "I suppose we are to wait here all day."

Lorrimer glanced about the room.

"Do you suppose there's a bell somewhere?" he asked, fretfully.

"What a question! Did you ever see a bell in a Japanese house?"

"The hotels all have them," he answered.

"This is not a hotel."

Lorrimer winced at her retorts. He said, a trifle apologetically:

"You see, my dear, the woman said she was dressing, or something like that."

"Then we may as well go back to Mr. Blount's. These Japanese women are inordinately vain, and spend hours in dressing."

"My daughter is not Japanese," said her husband, mildly.

The woman pursed her lips.

"I wonder what you really expect to see, Dick?" she said, looking at him curiously. "You're all unstrung."

Just then Aoi appeared at the door. She came towards them in a state of repressed excitement, and she welcomed her guests with stammering and uncertain words, though she courtesied so repeatedly that the visitors became uneasy.

"My daughter?" inquired Lorrimer, as soon as Aoi had ceased her kowtowing.

"She will come in a moment. The illustrious ones will pardon the child's nervousness."

"It is only natural," said Lorrimer, quietly, biting his underlip in his own restlessness.

Aoi's face, with its humble smile, suddenly appeared alert. She seemed to be listening.

"Ah, now she is coming, augustness," she said, as she crossed to the doors and slowly pushed them aside.

The Lorrimers had not heard the soft patter of the little feet in the matted hall, for a Japanese girl's tread in the house is almost soundless. Hence, when Aoi drew the sliding-doors apart, they had not expected to see the girl on the very threshold.

They started, simultaneously, at sight of the little figure. With drooping head, Hyacinth softly entered the room. At first glance she seemed no different from any other Japanese girl, save that she was somewhat taller. She was dressed in kimono and obi, her hair freshly arranged and shining in its smooth butterfly mode. Her face was bent to the floor, so that they could scarcely see more than its outline.

She hesitated a moment before them; then, as though unaware of the impetuous motion towards her of the man she knew was her father, she subsided to the mats and bowed her head at his feet.

The silence that ensued was painful.

Then Mrs. Lorrimer gasped, hysterically:

"This is not—not she?"

Lorrimer stooped gently down to the little figure and lifted her to her feet. She raised her face, and for a moment these two whose lives were so strangely connected looked into each other's faces. The father could not speak for some time, so intense were the emotions that assailed him. When he did find his voice, it was broken and trembling.

"My—my dear little daughter!" he said.

Then he bent and kissed her. She stood still, almost stonily, under his caress, but she did not return his embrace. She quietly withdrew her hands from his.

"It is unnatural—horrible," said Mrs. Lorrimer, beneath her breath. Low as was her voice, it broke the spell of silence, which rested like a pall in the room. Lorrimer turned to her quietly.

"And this," he said to Hyacinth, "is your—your mother."

She turned her eyes slowly upon the woman, and looked at her steadily. Then she said, in clear English:

"You make mistake. My mother is dead."

Again an embarrassed silence and constraint fell upon them all. This time it was Aoi who broke it. She turned her head from them as she spoke.

"Little one, it is your duty to accept the Engleesh lady as your mother."

For the first time the girl's unnatural calmness deserted her. She ran to Aoi, throwing her arms passionately about her.

"No, no," she cried. "You are the only mother I know. I will never have another. No!"

"What are they saying to each other?" asked Mrs. Lorrimer, watching them curiously.

"My knowledge of Japanese is limited," said her husband, heavily.

234

"The whole thing's a farce," she said.

"Do you find it so?" he asked, smiling bitterly.

"Oh, Dick, we can't be expected to understand a girl—like that."

"She is my daughter," was his quiet reply; and there was a new dignity in his voice.

"Yes, but she is different from us, so utterly alien. Just look at her. Would any one believe she was your daughter?"

He looked over at the little figure now soothing the weeping Aoi, and his wife's words found a hollow echo within him.

"Yet," said Mrs. Lorrimer, thoughtfully, "she is still very young and quite pretty. A few years in the West may make a great change in her. Who knows, we may make quite a little civilized modern out of her yet. She is Richard Lorrimer's daughter."

As though she knew they were talking about her, Hyacinth left Aoi and came

235

towards them, though she was careful to keep at a distance.

"Will my honorable father excuse our presence for to-day?" she said, in English.

"But you are going with us at once," said Mrs. Lorrimer.

With a movement that in a Western girl would have seemed rudeness, Hyacinth turned her back slowly towards her step-mother and addressed her words solely to her father.

"If it please you, august father," she said, "will you not deign to permit me to remain here with my—my friends till the time comes to leave Sendai?"

Her form of speech hurt her father strangely. He watched her face—unloving, emotionless, it seemed, when turned to his—and his own grew wistful. He was more than anxious to indulge her.

"Yes, yes, certainly," he said. "I appreciate your feelings. By all means

236

stay here if you wish. How long before—"

"Will you not permit me to remain
one month?" she said, somewhat timidly, and her eyes suddenly fell. She
could not tell why, but a flood of
emotions seemed to fill her heart, so that
she could no longer contain herself if
she must look into the face of her
father.

"We expected to leave at once," he
said, gently; "but if it is your wish to
remain longer, understand, I want you
to have your desires gratified."

She went towards him falteringly a
few steps. She held out her hands uncertainly.

He took them quickly in his own.
She raised her face to his, and suddenly
her eyes became blinded with tears; but,
when he stooped to kiss her, she slipped
to the floor at his feet.

He clasped his slender, nervous hands
together and looked down at the queer
little figure, now seeming to bow to him

after the strange fashion of the Japanese in bidding adieu. Then he turned to his wife.

"We had better go now," he said, huskily.

XXVIII

On an early morning in the month
of August, two young people were drift-
ing in a light sail-boat in and out of the
waters surrounding the rock islands of
Matsushima. They might have been
new lovers, they were so silent, and always they were gazing into each other's
faces, flushing and trembling when their
eyes met.

The boy, for he seemed still very
young, was graceful, and of grave,
sombre beauty. He was tall and dark,
and the expression of his deep-brown
eyes was tender and piercing. His
limbs were well formed, and his strong
arms, as he handled the boat, showed
that he was no mean athlete. He was
dressed in a gray hakama, the sleeves
rolled back. His head was bare, and the

wind, lifting the soft, dark locks, showed his high, fine brow.

The girl was small. Her hair, though brown, had a strangely sunny sheen to it, and her eyes were gray-blue, dreamy, and wistful. Koma, as he watched the changing expressions of her face, thought her fairer and lovelier than all the women of the great world he had seen.

There was a little padded seat in the boat, and against this she leaned back, trailing her hand in the still water, and watching now the sky, now the bay, now the hills on either side, and sometimes Komazawa.

They drifted about the bay in this silent, thrilling fashion for some time; then she suddenly spoke. Koma dropped the oar and sat forward.

"Do you know what the days seem like to me now?" she asked.

"No," he said, his eyes wandering inconstantly over her face.

"They are like a lotos bloom," she

said, "always pink and gold, and so beautiful that they are sure to fade."

For a moment he did not reply, then, leaning on his oar, he said:

"And if the day must fade, will not the morrow be as beautiful?"

"Ah, no," she said, sadly; "besides, we are not acquainted with the morrow. We only know the to-day, and so the heart breaks at the thought of parting from what is with us now."

"You are sad to-day. Yesterday you were merry."

"I was not merry at heart," she said, plaintively. "You are very clever, Koma, but, ah, you do not know everything."

He watched her face in silence.

"You think because I laugh and say gay things that my heart, too, is light."

"No, I do not think that," he said, earnestly; "but why should you not be happy and gay? You are only a maiden. You cannot know tears yet—little one." He added the old, familiar term

241

"little one" so softly that she strained her ears to hear it.

She held a lotos blossom close to her face, and looked down into its heart.

"See," she said, holding it towards him, "there is one drop of dew in the heart of the lotos. It is like a tear. It, too, poor flower, must fade away with the summer."

"Why do you say 'it, too'?"

"Like me," she said; "I will not be here when the summer has passed." Her voice broke. "You said I should not go. Yet—yet the days pass so swiftly. Only one week more—and—after that—? Ah, I cannot bear to think of it."

"Do you, then, love this Japan of ours so dearly?"

She looked about her, her eyes filled with tears. She clasped her little hands together.

"Ah, yes," she said.

"And you would not even be content

to go to the home of your ancestors for
—for a little while?"

"I am afraid," she said, simply—
"afraid to leave the land of gods and go
out into the unknown. It is the unknown that has such horror for me.
And the great seas are flat and bottom-
less. I could not have courage to cross
them unless I were forced to do so."

"But you would not be afraid to
cross them with me, would you, little
one?"

"No—not with you, Koma," she said,
looking into his eyes.

Leaning across, he took one of her
little hands, held it a space between
both his own, then lifted it to his lips.

"Never was there such faith as yours,
and in one—one who is not worthy to
touch you."

"When you talk like that, Koma," she
said, with tears in her voice, "you make
me sadder still, because when I am gone
from you I must recall those words."

"Then if such words make you sad, I

243

will not speak them again. Nothing but joy and sunshine should dwell in your face. So let us talk of happier things. See how near to the shore we are coming. Shall we land?"

"No. Let us drift on."

"Look how the sunbeams are gliding down the pine trunks. See how they, too, have tinted the green leaves to gold."

"There are no — no pine-trees in America. No more— And there are no sunbeams there. The sensei told me so."

"The sensei is ignorant. The sun is generous. He scatters his gifts all over the world."

"But he favors Nippon."

"Yes," he repeated, "he favors Nippon—all nature does so."

"And that America is cold."

"It has its summers, little one."

"Look," she said; "see, there is a little white fox on the hill there. It is looking at us. Ah, it is gone!"

"That is a good omen, is it not?" said Koma, smiling.

"Oh, surely. The foxes are sacred. Every one believes so except the mission-house people."

"We do not belong to the mission-house. We will believe so."

"How cheerful you are, Koma. You are not sorry to see me go?"

"You are not gone yet."

"But there is only one week left," she said, "and despair craves company. Do you, therefore, give me your sympathy?"

"Wait till the week is gone," he said, "and then if you still wish it, none will be sadder with you than I."

XXIX

A few days later. It is early evening
and the crickets are making a great
bustle in the grasses, while a small, gray
ape, swinging in a bamboo, is mingling
its chattering with the cawing of the
crows in the camphor-trees.

"Summer is passing," said Hyacinth,
"for everything is complaining."

"I do not complain," said Koma.

"No; life will always be summer for
you. You are not going away from
Nippon."

"Are you?" he asked.

"There is no help for me," she said.
"I grow more melancholy each day."

"Is it only Japan you care about
leaving?"

"Japan holds all—all that is dear to
me."

246

"And can you enumerate them—the things that are dear to you?"

She shook her head drearily.

"No," she said, "I cannot."

"Yet you could stay here if you wished."

"No. How could I?"

"Did not that young American from the consulate in Tokyo ask you to marry him? He lives here in Japan, necessarily."

She laughed.

"Was he not kind?" she said.

"Why did you refuse him?"

"Oh, for many reasons."

"Tell me them."

"He belongs to the West country, after all."

"He does not think so. For your sake he would forswear even that."

"Ah, but he does so, nevertheless. The gods—no, his God—fashioned him for his own land."

"And was that the only reason why you refused him?"

247

"No. I do—do not—" She hesitated, and turned her head droopingly from him. "I do not love him," she said, simply.

"You did not love Yamashiro Yoshida, yet you would have married him."

"I did not know better," she said, faintly.

"But it is only a little while since."

"A month," she said; "since you returned."

"Confess to me," he said, his eyes gleaming, "that it was I who made you know the meaning of love, and I will tell you why you are not going to America to-morrow—no, nor the day after, nor until you shall go with me."

"What can I confess?" she said, tremulously. "I do not know what you wish, dear Koma." She was trembling now.

"Confess to me," he said, "else I cannot speak, for fear I should wrong you, my little one. I will not try to urge you to stay here—with me—unless—"

248

"I—I cannot speak," she said. "I know not what to say."

"Then I will speak," he said. "I love you, I love you, Hyacinth; with all the life that throbs within me, I love you. Do you understand? No, do not speak unless you can answer my heart with your own. I want you for my own. Ah, I know I have won you! It is not a delusion, for I see it in your eyes, your lips. You do not know it yet, you are so innocent and pure, but I—ah, I am sure of it!"

She raised her quivering face to his in the moonlight. Then suddenly her head fell upon her clasped hands.

"Ah, is this—love?" she said.

He lifted her face and kissed her lips, her eyes, then her little, trembling hands.

"This is love—and this, and this."

Later they came to a hidden path arched on either side by the drooping bamboos. The moon was above them, making a silver pathway for their feet.

249

"Whither do we go?" she tremulously whispered.

"I know the way," said he, gently leading her onward.

They came to an open space, a narrow field. And on the grass, the winds, gently blowing, moved back and forth in the moonlight strange wisps of white paper.

"It is the Path of Prayer," said Koma.

She understood, and was dumb with the thrilling of her emotions.

"Here," he said, "the Goddess of Mercy walks nightly. Though we are no longer sad, let us leave our prayer here among these sad petitions for her to read."

"Yes," she said, " and we will pray to Kuannon for those less fortunate than we."

Kneeling there in the silver light, they wrote on fragments of paper their simple prayers. Did the Heavenly Lady, when trailing her robes of mercy through the Path of Prayer, read also the petitions of the lovers?

They left the Path of Prayer and climbed to the summit of the hill. Softly they turned their feet towards the mission-house.

"We have said our prayers to Kuannon—now we will turn to the God of our fathers," he whispered.

They paused a moment on the missionary's doorstep. She raised her face to his.

"The Reverend Blount may refuse," she said.

"He will not," he assured her, "since he has promised me. Come!"

THE END